The Daughter-In-Law Syndrome

By

Stevie Turner

The Daughter-In-Law Syndrome

All names and characters are fictitious. Any similarity to persons living or deceased is purely coincidental.

Thanks to LLPix Designs and Obsessed by Books Designs for the cover.

Dedication

Dedicated to all daughters-in-law everywhere.

Table of Contents

SYNOPSIS

The Daughter-in-law Syndrome delves into the complicated relationship that is causing much friction between Grandmother Edna Deane and her daughter-in-law Arla. In addition it focuses on the sometimes tumultuous partnership between Arla and her husband Ric.

Arla Deane sometimes likens her marriage to undergoing daily psychological warfare. Husband Ric will never voice an opinion, and puts his mother Edna up high on a pedestal. Arla is sick of always feeling that she comes in at only second best to her mother-in-law, who much to Arla's fury is never told anything by Ric or his sisters that she would not want to hear.

This novel explores the husband/wife, mother/son, and mother-in-law/daughter-in-law relationships. After twenty eight years of marriage, Arla, the daughter-in-law, is at the end of her tether and persuades a reluctant Ric to accompany her for marriage guidance. As they look back over their lives with Counsellor Toni Beecher, Arla slowly comes to realise her own failings, and eventually discovers the long-hidden reason why Ric will never utter a cross word to his mother.

Also, adding to Arla's stress is the fact that her son Stuart will soon be marrying Ria, a girl whom Arla feels is just looking for a free ride. Arla is convinced that Ria will be no asset to Stuart at all; her new daughter-in-law just wants to be a mother and has no intention of ever working again once the babies start to arrive. After visiting Stuart and Ria for Sunday lunch, Arla is convinced that her son is making the biggest mistake of his life!

PROLOGUE

IRENE FENTON LOOKED into the dark, fathomless depths of her seven-year-old daughter's eyes.

"Why is Millie crying?"

"She really, really wanted to play with my favourite dolly, but I said no." Arla shook her head for added emphasis.

"She's come here to see you; I want you to give her a dolly to play with."

"No; they're all mine. She can't play with any of them."

Irene sighed.

"If you do not give Millie one of your dolls to play with, you will not be going to the cinema on Saturday morning."

"But she'll break it!" Arla's eyes filled with tears.

"She will do no such thing. You have to learn to share." Irene wondered not for the first time if she should have had more than one child.

"I don't like sharing." Arla stamped her foot to emphasise her point.

"There are things in life we have to do even though we don't want to do them. You'll make Millie happy if you share one of your dolls with her, and she's more likely to come back to play again."

"Millie can't play with any of my things." Arla stood in front of her mother, wilful and defiant. "They're *mine*."

"Then nobody will like you, and you'll have no friends." Irene's voice rose. "I'm going to phone Millie's mother now to come and collect her, and you can spend the rest of the day in your bedroom."

Arla, head held high, stomped with feeling to her room. All around her on the floor were her collection of dolls and teddies, and also a beautiful pink and purple doll's house that her father had recently painted. She wanted to gather all her toys close to her chest and keep them there; how could her mother even suggest that she lend Millie one of her treasured dolls to play with?

She sat quietly talking to her dolls until she realised she was hungry. She looked up at the clock on the wall; the big hand pointed to twelve, and the little hand pointed to the number five. She could smell something cooking downstairs, and her mouth started to water. Inching open the bedroom door, she stepped out onto the landing and looked over the bannister. She could hear the radio blaring away in the kitchen, and her mother singing as she fried something in a pan.

"Can I have some dinner please?" She shouted to get over the noise of the radio.

"Selfish, jealous girls do not deserve any dinner." Irene came out into the hallway and looked up. "Go back into your room and think about being nice to Millie."

"I'm sorry, Mummy." Arla whined. "I'm not selfish; I'm not jealous!"

"Then give me one of your dolls that Millie can play with next time, if indeed she wants to come back again, and I will make sure she plays with it. Actually, to be honest, I don't blame her if she doesn't want to come back." Irene wiped her hands on her apron.

"I'll get one now!"

Arla ran back into her room and picked out her worst doll, the one whose hair was starting to fall out. With some reluctance she presented it to her mother in the kitchen, trying not to salivate at the aroma of frying onions.

"I'm hungry, Mummy."

"Go back upstairs; you can have some dinner in your room."

Pleased that her mother had relented on one issue at least, Arla sat down again in front of her toys. She looked around her and suddenly wished Millie was still there; they could have played together with her new doll's house. Playing Mummies and Daddies on her own was not turning out to be as much fun as she had first thought.

CHAPTER 1

"HOW LONG HAVE the two of you been married?"

Arla's nose was irritated by a pungent aroma emanating from two smoking joss sticks perched in a plant pot at a rakish angle. She sniffed and looked up from the carpet with its many dog hairs towards the friendly smile worn by Antoinette Beecher, and waited for her husband Ric to say something; *anything*. However, Ric was remaining as silent as the proverbial tomb.

"Twenty eight years, and we'd known each other a year before the wedding." Arla nodded towards Ric to confirm her statement.

"And has the marriage been generally happy up until now?" Toni Beecher wondered if pulling teeth would be easier than trying to make this couple open up.

"We've had our ups and downs, as does anyone, but now I've finally decided that we can't go on like we have been, and that something needs to change."

"Something?" Toni asked.

"Well….er… *someone* more like." Arla replied and looked at Ric, confident in the knowledge that the 'someone' was not going to be herself.

Toni briefly wondered if the morose man sitting opposite her and trying to shut out the world, was in fact mute.

"What would you both like to get out of these sessions?" Arla thought carefully before replying.

"Perhaps you can get out of Ric why he'll never voice an opinion on any subject, and why he'll never tell his mother anything that she doesn't want to hear."

"And you, Mr Deane? What are you looking for here?" Toni smiled as pleasantly as she could, and strived for eye contact.

Concentrating her gaze on the tassels fringing the moth-eaten rug under the coffee table, and with a growing disappointment at her husband's continuing silence, Arla then looked up and let her eyes stray about the room towards the counsellor's overflowing bookshelves, trying to catch a glimpse of their obscure titles. When her eyes did focus on a book's spine, she realised that the wording on it made absolutely no sense to her whatsoever.

"So…..what problems have brought you both to see me today?" Toni changed the subject and again tried for eye contact from either one, but gave up.

"There aren't any problems as far as I'm concerned." Ric cleared his throat and shifted about uneasily on the sofa. "I'm fine; life goes on as always, doesn't it? It was Arla who suggested we do this; I'm not really sure *what* the problem is."

"Only because you can't see what's going on right in front of your nose." Arla looked at her husband and nervously twisted her wedding ring around with the forefinger and thumb of her right hand.

"Mrs Deane, would you care to elaborate a little bit please?" Toni was relieved to have heard Ric Deane's deep, resonant voice.

Arla was soothed by the seemingly young-looking counsellor's velveteen voice and unfaltering smile. Strands of dark fringe touched her eyes, and she pushed them away impatiently.

"As I said before, it's his bloody mother. For years I've put up with it, but no more. He doesn't want to admit there's a problem. The woman is slowly but surely ruining us." Arla wiped away a stray tear and sighed.

"Mr Deane, would you like to comment on your wife's statement?" Toni jotted down some notes whilst waiting for a reply.

Arla heard Ric's familiar ritual of pre-utterance throat-clearing, and braced herself for the answer.

"She doesn't understand; I'm piggy-in-the-middle here. She doesn't fall out with her own mother, and I don't want to argue with mine. Mum's getting on a bit now, and it's my job to look after her. She's not too well these days, and the last thing I want is to cause her any stress." Ric ran a hand quickly through his greying dark hair.

The sound of a ticking clock was deafening in the silence of the room. Arla swallowed her anger and waited for the next question.

"I always advise couples that a good marriage is all about trust and open communication. I encourage both parties to set aside time to talk to each other about their problems. If you're finding it difficult to speak about what's bothering you to me, then I suggest maybe pick half an hour about three times a week where you can talk privately at home and focus on your issues."

"I've tried that, and it doesn't work." Arla shook her head. "We need to speak with *you* about it. That's why we've come here."

"Okay, well of course I'm here to help." Toni put down her pen and looked Arla. "For this first session then I'll ask you, Mrs Deane, to speak first and for your husband to listen. Hopefully you'll be able to discuss things more when you get home, and when you come back later in the week then your husband will get the chance to talk uninterruptedly."

Arla nodded in agreement:

"That sounds fair."

"Would you like to begin then?" Toni Beecher gave what she thought was an encouraging look.

"Where do I start?" Arla shrugged her shoulders. "I don't know."

"At the beginning." Said Toni with a smile. "It's always a good place."

CHAPTER 2

"MUM, THIS IS my girlfriend Arla; Arla, meet my mum Edna."

"Hello; pleased to meet you."

Arla smiled and waited for some acknowledgement of her statement. There was none. The middle-aged, greying woman in front of her avoided eye contact altogether.

"Richard, where have you been? We were supposed to be going to Val and Ronnie's for tea this afternoon." Edna's visage was grim, as she looked past Arla to her son.

"Oh, sorry, I forgot; we've been out shopping. We can go now if you like; it'll be an ideal opportunity for Arla to meet them."

Arla wanted to fade into the wallpaper on hearing Ric's attempt to smooth things over.

"Oh no, I wouldn't want to put anyone out." Arla shook her head.

"You won't; Val won't be eating this early anyway." Ric looked at his watch. "I'll start the car up again; come on Mum, put your coat on."

The silence in the car was almost palpable. Arla was aware that Ric was driving faster than normal, but was not sure if it was due to feeling angry at his mother's treatment of her, or whether he was keen to get to his sister's house without too much more delay.

"Hello! You're dead on time!" Val Braithwaite, exquisitely groomed as usual, stood at the front door and glanced at Arla whilst addressing her brother. "Who's this?"

Arla felt like a fish out of water, but smiled maniacally, all the while conscious that Edna had not yet even acknowledged her or directed one word towards her. She was grateful to suddenly feel Ric's arm around her shoulders.

"This is my girlfriend Arla; Arla this is my sister Val."

"Arla? Unusual name!" Val looked at Arla with interest.

"My dad always liked Woody Guthrie's music. Woody had a son called Arlo I think, but they couldn't call me Arlo because I was a girl." Arla was aware she was gabbling inanely with nerves.

"Really?" Val appeared unimpressed. "Well, come in; there's plenty to eat."

"Thank you. I'm glad we're not late." She hoped her last remark would not go unnoticed by Edna.

Arla was grateful for the noise generated at the tea table by Val's two boisterous sons, who looked at her with unbridled curiosity. She watched Edna silently chomping mechanically on corned beef and pickle sandwiches and sending her daughter knowing glances, and wondered just what she had done to be ignored and treated so rudely.

"Where do you work, Arla?" Val supervised her sons' table manners at the same time as nibbling on a bird portion of food herself.

"At the Westen hospital; I'm a nurse."

"Is that so? We're always up there when one or other of the boys have got bits dropping off. I've never seen you."

"I work on one of the geriatric wards." Arla could not help simultaneously shooting Edna one of her hard stares.

"God; I could never do that." Val wrinkled her nose. "All that wee and poop."

"I find it quite rewarding actually." Arla took a piece of Victoria sponge. "Thanks for the tea Val; this cake looks delicious."

"Richard will do his usual job of polishing any leftovers off, so get in there quick."

"You make me sound as though I'm some sort of gannet." Ric took another sandwich. "All the same, if there's cake going spare, I'm there!"

Arla listened to the good-natured banter batting back and forth between brother and sister, but wanted to be far away. She felt invisible in Edna's presence, and as the meal progressed she became more and more morose. The only saving grace was a ring on the doorbell.

"Mum; keep an eye on Ben and Mark for a minute." Val stood up.

"Okay." Edna sipped tea from a mug and appeared unconcerned.

The boys looked aghast to be under their grandmother's watchful eye. Arla saw Ben sidle off the chair and go towards the front door, returning holding his mother's hand and also the hand of a stouter black-haired clone of Val whom she did not recognise.

"Jan, meet Richard's girlfriend Arla. Arla, this is my younger sister Jan, but not more beautiful I might add." Val gave a trilling laugh.

"Hello." Arla turned around. "Pleased to meet you."

"Likewise I'm sure." Jan smiled. "Any tea left for me?"

"Pull up another chair; I think Richard might have left you a sandwich."

Arla listened with half an ear to Ric and his sisters chatting away about nothing in particular. She smiled at the boys whilst realising with horror that nerves had made her consume six sandwiches and three pieces of cake. Edna remained monosyllabic.

Later on as she snuggled next to Ric on the back seat of his car out of sight of her mother's twitching net curtains, she put her arms around him and sighed.

"I don't think your mother liked me; she didn't speak one word to me all the afternoon." She boiled at the injustice of it.

"I never noticed; I'm sure she must have said something to you?" Ric looked at her incredulously.

"No; not a word. Have you ever brought other girls home to meet her? Did she speak to them okay?" Arla nibbled his neck, pleased for the chance to discover where she stood in Ric's estimation.

"You're the first one because you're special. In fact you're so special, that I want to ask you a question."

"What?" She looked up at him with interest.

"If I bought you an engagement ring, would you wear it?" He swallowed, grabbed her tight, and held his breath.

Arla sat up, flabbergasted:

"Ric, is this a proposal?" Her heart started to race with excitement.

"Sure is; what do you say? Will you marry me? I love you so much!"

"Yes, yes, and yes again!"

She lost herself in his kiss, all thoughts of Edna temporarily relegated to the back burner.

She thought it was impossible to be any happier than she was. As Ric drove her home, she had a fleeting thought.

"Do you think your mum will be pleased when she finds out we're getting married?"

"Does it matter *what* she thinks?" Ric glanced at Arla briefly. "*I* love you; if she doesn't like it then she can lump it."

"Yes, but *will* she like it?" Arla felt uneasiness creeping in at hearing Ric's reply.

"I'm sure she'll fall in love with you, just as I have."

"What about your sisters? Do you think they liked me?" Arla wondered if she would ever match Val's elegant poise and self-assurance.

"Why wouldn't they? You worry too much." Ric put a hand on her knee briefly. "You're a beautiful woman; I love you."

"I love you too." Arla sighed. "I just want your family to feel the same way."

"They will; give them time." Ric replied confidently.

CHAPTER 3

SHE COULD SEE their three dark heads bent together in conversation as Ric smooched her around the dance floor. She had already thought of a name for them……*The Three Witches of Westen*……

"Happy?" He looked down at her from his grand height of six feet four inches.

"Absolutely!" She gazed up at his dark eyes and grinned. Placing her hands in a good position on Ric's shoulders, Arla watched with satisfaction as her diamond engagement ring glinted in the myriad of silvery shards emanating from a mirror ball above. She glanced momentarily over his shoulder and caught Edna's eye, who was seated in a corner and flanked by her two expressionless daughters. Edna had managed to keep up the eye contact with an inscrutable expression on her face, whilst mouthing something to her daughters over Stevie Wonder's new song.

"I just called to say I love you!" Ric, tone deaf but totally unaware of the fact, gazed into Arla's eyes and consistently sang a semitone flat with gusto.

Arla could see Val and Jan, the two henchwomen, looking in her direction whilst smirking a reply to their mother, and suddenly wished she had learned how to lip read.

"I just called to say how much I care!" Ric kissed the top of her head.

"I wonder what your sisters are laughing about?" Arla shrugged off a stab of irritation as she threw what she hoped was a suitably knowing look towards them.

"Who knows? Who cares?" He pulled her to him. "What I do know is that I love you very much."

She buried her face in his warm shirt-front, which now smelt of cigarette smoke:

"Mmm.... Love you too."

When the song ended she saw Val stand up and head over in their direction:

"Richard! You haven't danced with me all evening!" Val pouted, threw back her shiny mane of black curls, and ignoring Arla, grabbed her brother's hand and dragged him towards the dance floor.

"Guess I'd better do something about that then!" Ric pulled a face. "Oh god, he's playing 'Wham!' now!"

Arla kept up a fixed smile whilst walking through the throng of sweaty dancers gyrating to 'Wake Me Up Before You Go-Go' while shouting out their congratulations, and found a spare seat next to her father.

"Not dancing, Dad?" She picked up his pint of bitter and took a few sips. "Yuck, that's horrible!" She pulled a face.

"I'm not dancing to those two poofs. Mum's shaking it about up there, but as you know I'm more your ballroom dancing man." Jimmy Fenton kept one eye on his wife Irene, as she twisted energetically on the dance floor.

"I'm having a great night; thanks for the party." Arla kissed her father's cheek.

"That's okay. It's not every day your only daughter gets engaged." Jimmy smiled and took a large swig of his pint. "Who's that woman Ric's dancing with?"

"His sister Val. I don't think she likes me much, and nor does Jan, the other one." Arla sighed.

"Why wouldn't they like you? You're the best thing that's ever happened to Ric, that's for certain." Jimmy nodded to confirm his statement.

"I don't know; there's something about his mother and sisters that I'm not sure about. They were looking daggers at me just now." Arla felt a surge of jealousy at the sight of Ric's arm around the back of Val's shimmering tiny red cocktail dress.

"Let them look, love. I know who the better girl is." Jimmy lifted his glass again. "Cheers!"

"Dad; don't you think it's strange that Ric's mother hardly ever says a word to me? D'you know what else she does? If I'm with him, she adds his name to the end of every question she asks, and so purposely leaves me out of the conversation." Arla followed Ric with her eyes.

"They seem a rum old lot, that's for sure, but your chap seems alright." Jimmy smiled at his daughter.

"He's lovely, it's just the rest of them I'm worried about." Arla shrugged.

"Forget them if you're happy with Ric; it's not the rest of his family you're marrying." Jimmy replied.

As the song finished Arla saw Ric extricate himself from his sister's clutches and make his way towards them.

"Hi Jimmy, not out there on the dance floor moving and grooving then?" Ric plonked himself down next to Arla and loosened his tie.

"Behave yourself. I'm alright here with my pint; don't you worry." Jimmy chuckled. "So when's the wedding going to be?"

"We don't know yet; sometime next year probably." Arla took Ric's hand in hers and gave it a squeeze.

"There's plenty of time; you're only twenty one. Don't rush to get bogged down with mortgages and babies." Jimmy shook his head.

"But we're in love, Dad." Arla shot Ric a shy glance.

"Ah, yeah. Love. I remember that." Jimmy's eyes searched the dance floor again.

"We'd best go and talk to Mum for a while." Ric pulled Arla to her feet. "Come on; she's sitting over there on her own now."

Reluctantly, she followed Ric to the other side of the hall, to where Edna Deane now resided in solitary splendour.

"Richard! I was wondering when you were coming over!" Edna patted the seat next to hers. "Come and sit down and keep me company."

Arla noticed there was no reference to herself at all, and stood there awkwardly until Ric pulled her down onto his lap and twirled a finger around a strand of her shoulder-length chestnut brown hair.

"Isn't my fiancée beautiful?" He looked at Arla, and then back at his mother.

"Yes." Edna answered half-heartedly as she looked at her daughters still tossing their tresses on the dance floor. "I assume you'll not be getting married too soon, Richard."

"We're saving for a deposit on a flat, so hopefully next year."

From Arla's sideways perch on Ric's lap, she found to her horror that her legs were almost touching Edna's. With his arms clamped around her middle, she twisted around to face the front.

"Val should have been a model. Look at her figure, Richard." Edna looked her daughter up and down approvingly. "A perfect size eight, even after two babies. It's a pity your father didn't live to see you all grown up."

"Dad would have loved you." Ric gave Arla a squeeze.

"When did your dad pass away?" Arla ignored Edna and turned towards Ric.

"Mr Deane died three years' ago." Edna's voice interrupted.

"You said that without moving your lips!" Arla chuckled and squeezed Ric's arms with her own.

"Could you get me another sherry please, Richard?" Edna fished in her purse for some change.

"Sure. I'll get it; put your money away."

He lifted Arla to her feet and she followed him over to the bar, unwilling to wait with Edna.

"Why does she always call you Richard, when everybody else calls you Ric?" Arla looked across the hall, conscious of Edna's eyes watching her every move.

"I don't know; my sisters do it as well. I prefer to be called Ric though; Richard sounds a bit poofy to me."

"Well, why don't you tell them all then?"

"Best not to rock the boat." Ric shrugged and sighed.

When the party finished Arla prepared herself for the next stage in the battle as she watched for a reaction on Edna's face to her son's statement.

"I'm going to run Arla home, Mum. Val and Ronnie said you can go with them."

"Surely she can go home with her own parents, can't she?" Edna looked past Arla to Ric.

"She could do, but I want to take her home." "Oh

well, I'll have to go with Val then, won't I?"

Arla was encouraged on hearing the revelation that now she had progressed to being a *she* in Edna's eyes. *At least it was an improvement to being nameless and invisible.*

CHAPTER 4

TONI BEECHER TURNED over a new page of her notebook.

"So, Mrs Deane, as far as you're concerned, the problems had started from day one?"

"Absolutely, and worse from the moment we became engaged certainly. Ric had been the only one left living at home, you see. His sisters were both older than him and were already married, and I suppose his mother realised that once Ric and I tied the knot then she would be left on her own."

"What happened next?" Toni picked up her pen.

Arla slipped her hand in Ric's, which seemed unresponsive.

"We decided it would take too long to save up for a mortgage; we wanted to be together, and so we rented a flat just outside Westen. Ric had finished his plumbing apprenticeship, and I was earning good money as a newly-qualified nurse. It was back in the early 'Eighties, and my family thought the whole scenario was a bit scandalous; us living together without being married, but at the time we just didn't care."

"You would have rather lived together and then save up for the wedding afterwards." Toni nodded in Arla's direction.

"Exactly." Arla squeezed Ric's hand.

"How did your mother-in-law cope with being on her own?"

"I once found out from his sisters that she had phoned around the whole family crying down the line and letting everyone know that Ric had moved out and had left her all alone. After a few weeks she then started getting on the bus and inviting herself round to our flat for dinner every Sunday. His sisters were at home looking after children during the week, and she would visit them on weekdays while we were out working. Unfortunately for us I think their husbands viewed weekends as sacrosanct, and it seemed that every Sunday, particularly when I wasn't working the early shift, without fail she would be knocking on our door at eleven o'clock in the morning. My parents would sometimes visit us on Saturday afternoons if I wasn't working, but it was never a regular thing with them." Arla sighed with the relief of getting her resentment out in the open.

"How did this affect your relationship?" Toni looked up from her notebook intently.

Without the usual words of condemnation from Ric, Arla felt encouraged to pour out her feelings to the counsellor.

"I thought that maybe she'd eventually get used to being on her own and stop coming round, but when I complained to Ric after about six months that we never spent a Sunday by ourselves, it was like talking to a brick wall."

"In what way?"

"He would pretend that the problem didn't exist."

Arla felt Ric's hand slide from hers, and out of the corner of her eye she saw him fold his arms defensively across his chest.

"Did he look forward to his mother's visits?"

"He never said, but I don't think so; we were young and in love, and sometimes we just wanted to lie in bed and have sex on a Sunday morning like thousands of other newlyweds, but we had to get up. I had to have dinner on the table by half past twelve, because I knew she'd be round, and that was the time she liked to eat her lunch."

"I see. What was the atmosphere like during these visits?"

Arla looked sideways at Ric, who kept his gaze fixed on a jug of water on the coffee table.

"Ric would laugh and joke with his mother as though everything was okay, but I'd be seething inside. I'd been brought up to eat healthily, and here our paths definitely diverged because of Edna's sweet tooth. For example, she would complain that I wasn't adding sugar to the saucepan of carrots, and always reminded me to baste fat from the beef over the roast potatoes." Arla took a deep breath. "When I once mentioned that we never ate chocolate biscuits because we didn't want to put on too much weight, Edna brought a bagful of them with her the following Sunday, just for Ric. As soon as she went home I threw them away. It annoys me that as far as she's concerned, *her* opinion is the only correct one. Woe betide anybody who thinks differently."

"You obviously do." Toni smiled and nodded her head.

"Yes, that's why we don't get along."

Arla was aware of Ric's pursed lips, crossed legs, and folded arms. She wondered how he had managed to stay quiet for so long.

"Anyway, to carry on, if I was working the early shift she'd still be there on a Sunday afternoon when I came home at three o'clock. Ric never learned how to cook, and so she would have taken over my kitchen and cooked him a roast dinner. My dinner would be cold on a plate. I could never eat it because the potatoes would be covered in fat, and the vegetables would all be swimming in congealed cheese up to their waists. She would bring her own cheese in her handbag just to spite me." Arla shuddered. "I told her countless times to stop cooking me a dinner, but she never took any notice. Ric failed to say one word of criticism to her, and the whole farce went on for years until I gave up work when our daughter Shelley come along." She looked up at the clock. "There's so much more I can tell you, but I can see our time's up now."

Toni Beecher finished writing a sentence and then closed her notebook:

"We've made a good start. I suggest it would be helpful for the two of you to take time out to discuss what's been said today, ready for the next session." Toni looked directly at Ric. "Mr Deane, we will hear your side of the story on Thursday; shall we say seven o'clock?"

Arla nodded in agreement as she handed over forty pounds, aware of no acknowledgement at all coming from her husband's direction. Twenty eight years of marriage had taught her one thing; her husband would not be able to walk away or avoid talking about the subject while they were driving home together in the car.

The February snow was just starting to ice over as they said their goodbyes to Toni Beecher and walked carefully along the frozen pavement. Arla switched on the seat warmers whilst they waited for the windscreen to de-mist.

"How do you think it went then?" She clipped her seat belt in place and kept her eyes focused on the car parked in front.

"Waste of forty quid if you ask me." Ric cleared his throat. "All the talking in the world isn't going to change the fact that you hate my mother."

"And she hates me too, don't forget." Arla could feel her face beginning to flush in anger.

"You've never let me forget. You've paid forty pounds and I'm still piggy-in-the-middle." Ric slammed his seat belt into the holder with undue force.

"Just for once it'd be good for you to stop being neutral, take my side for a change, and offer me a little bit of support. I'm your wife for God's sake!"

When Ric started up the car and sped off on the ice like a demon possessed, Arla closed her eyes and prayed that they were going to make it home in one piece. However, experience told her to keep her opinion on Ric's driving to herself. She knew that if she even tentatively mentioned the fact that he was driving much too fast, her contrary husband would then slow down to under 10 miles per hour for the rest of the journey, and it would take them hours upon hours to get home. *No, she thought, best to say nothing. She had made that calamitous mistake once before…..*

CHAPTER 5

IF THEY RAN quickly enough they could leg it around the corner before the old girl got to the front door. Ric, hopping from foot to foot in excitement, decided to let Ronnie Braithwaite push the doorbell this time.

"I can hear somebody! Quick!" Ronnie glanced quickly at Ric before speeding down the road like a scalded cat.

Ric, the heavier of the two, made the mistake of looking over his shoulder before turning the corner. Mrs Osborne stood on her step shaking her fist:

"I'll be letting your mothers know what you've been up to!"

"Shit!" Ric, giggling, fell puffing and panting upon the grass verge, and punched Ronnie in the back. "I told you not to go back to that one!"

"She won't do anything." Ronnie, breathing evenly, sat up straight again and pulled up his socks. "When we go back home I dare you to knock on her door one more time."

"Fuck off; you do it."

There was no sign of anything untoward as Ric, stomach growling with hunger, said goodbye to Ronnie some time later and let himself in at the back door.

"Where have you been? Tea's nearly ready." Edna Deane took an apple pie out of the oven and smiled down upon her ten year old son.

"Out with Ronnie."

"What about your homework?"

"I've done it."

"No he hasn't, Mum; his satchel's still in the hallway." Janet Deane came into the kitchen and poked her tongue out at her brother.

"Jan's been too busy kissing Adie Michaels in the garden to notice whether I've done it or not!" Ric stuck his middle finger up at Janet behind his mother's back.

"I was not!" Janet's face turned the colour of a cooked beetroot.

Edna wiped her hands on her apron.

"Put a sock in it the pair of you! Go and see who that is ringing the doorbell."

Janet, three years older and somewhat faster, made the front door in record time. Ric's heart sank at the sight of Mary Osborne.

"Can I speak to your mother please,

Janet." "Sure; I'll go and get her."

Ric dived into the dining room out of sight of the old woman's accusing eyes. He heard his mother's footsteps going towards the open front door.

"Mrs Deane; I have to let you know that your boy keeps knocking on my door and running away. I caught him at it again this afternoon. There was another boy with him; a few years older, but not so heavily built."

"You must be mistaken. Richard has been home all day with me. He's got a stomach ache."

Edna's voice was firm. Ric relaxed, sidled out from behind the door, and took the top piece of buttered bread from a plate on the dining room table.

"You little shit!" Janet whispered at her brother as she took her place next to him. "You always get away with everything!"

Ric thanked the good Lord above, the Queen, the Duke of Edinburgh, and Uncle Tom Cobleigh and all that his father had not yet returned home from work. He kicked Janet under the table and smiled at his mother as she brought the still-steaming apple pie into the dining room.

"This is for pudding. Dad's working late, so we'll save him a piece."

"Can I have two bits?" Ric's mouth watered as the smell of the pie assailed his nostrils.

"We'll see." His mother's conspiratorial grin was reassuring.

If only he could turn back the clock. Ric struggled to bring his mind back to the present, and tried to concentrate on what was being said in the hot, stuffy room:

"Mr Deane, I'm going to give you the stage today, but firstly I just wondered if you and your wife had managed to talk at all about what was discussed last time?" Toni Beecher shuffled a few papers, and picked up her notebook and pen.

"Not really. It doesn't work; we only end up arguing." Ric, decidedly ill-at-ease, looked down at his boots.

"I see. If our sessions are going to work for you, then you will both have to talk to each other about what we discuss here; otherwise not much will be gained."

"Yeah, okay." Ric sighed, uncrossed, and then re-crossed his ankles.

The counsellor took the protective cover off the top of her pen:

"Mr Deane, how would you describe family life as you were growing up? Did you get on well with your parents?"

Ric nodded tersely:

"Yeah. I argued with my sisters sometimes, but then who doesn't?" He shrugged.

"Just childish squabbles I take it?" Toni looked at him with interest.

"Of course. Mum would usually intervene and sort us out."

"Where was your father in all this? You haven't mentioned him." Toni jotted down a sentence in her notebook.

"He did shift work; we didn't see him much. He worked for British Rail as a train driver."

"I see. So your mother ran the home and was your main carer most of the time?"

"Yeah, I suppose so." He sighed with irritation. "Dad would take me to see Westen Albion play when they were at home, or he'd help me fix my bike, but most of the time I went to Mum if there were any problems."

"And you felt close to your mum?" Toni chewed the end of her pen thoughtfully.

"Yeah, I suppose so; doesn't any kid?"

"Not necessarily. It depends on the kind of relationship between the mother and child."

"Well, we weren't a dysfunctional family if that's what you're getting at. Mum had a bit of a temper, but if you kept on the right side of her she was a piece of cake."

"Could you elaborate a bit more on the last sentence please?" Toni smiled. "Was your mother quite fiery then?"

"Yeah, she could be, but not usually with me once I found out how to get round her. Mum and my eldest sister Val had a few ding dongs when Val started going out with boyfriends and staying out late, especially when she ended up getting engaged to my best mate Ronnie, but I knew how to keep on her right side."

"How did you do that?" Toni looked at Ric intently.

"Well, basically I'd butter her up and tell her what she wanted to hear. Val wasn't so subtle, but Jan and I had it sussed." Ric shrugged.

"Did that entail lying sometimes?"

"Yeah, I'd say quite a few times actually." Ric chuckled. "Ronnie eventually won her over though. She thinks the sun shines out of his backside now."

Toni let a thin smile play about her lips.

"What would have happened if you hadn't lied?"

"Then World War Three would have broken out. I tried it a few times, but soon learned it was easier to keep the peace."

Arla, up until now quiescent, suddenly turned around to face Ric on the sofa:

"Can't you see you're still doing this? You're a grown man and you're still telling her what she wants to hear!"

Toni shifted her gaze across the sofa.

"Mrs Deane; today is your husband's story. At the next session you will both be able to talk."

"Sorry." Arla, frustrated, let out a breath and sank back in her seat.

"Mr Deane, on the times that World War Three broke out, how did your relationship with your mother change?" Toni recommenced chewing the end of her pen.

"She wouldn't speak to me for weeks." Ric sighed and fiddled with a button on his cuff.

"She cut you dead?"

"Yeah."

"How did that make you feel?"

"I was just a kid. Frightened I suppose. Val gave as good as she got and sometimes they never spoke for months at a time, but it used to affect me. I didn't like arguments."

"How about now? How do arguments with your wife affect you?"

Ric undid the button on his cuff, and then re-buttoned it while he thought of a reply:

"I don't like arguing. We only usually have disagreements over my mother. Most of the time I'm pretty easy-going. As I said before, it's better to keep the peace as far as Mum's concerned."

"Because even though you're an adult, she still wouldn't talk to you anymore if you argued?" Toni looked quizzically in Ric's direction.

"I suppose so, but she's a little old lady now; I look after her and keep her sweet."

"You must love her very much."

"Yeah; who knows? Maybe I do." Ric shrugged as the button on his cuff fell to the floor.

"Mr Deane, how did your mother react when you first announced your engagement?" Toni Beecher gazed directly over at Ric to gauge his expression.

"I don't really remember; it was too long ago." Ric yawned and sighed.

"Did she appear pleased?"

"I expect so. It's a happy occasion, isn't it?"

"Were you worried about telling her the happy news?"

"No; I don't think so. Look, what's our getting engaged got to do with anything? Can we change the subject?"

"Mr Deane, unless you are willing to elaborate more on my questions, it's going to be quite difficult for me to suggest any therapies for you and your wife to undertake." Toni Beecher gave Ric a smile that did not quite reach her eyes. "Would you like to stop for today and try again next time?"

"You bet your bottom dollar I would." Ric stood up, ready to go. "Lady, you're a mind reader."

CHAPTER 6

THERE WAS ONLY a small space between them in the bed, but as far as Arla was concerned, it may just as well have been a chasm.

"You've never said anything before about your mum not talking to you when you were a kid."

"You've never asked."

"Well, I'm asking now."

"I don't want to talk about it. It doesn't get us anywhere; let's just knock it on the head for tonight. This whole thing is beginning to get on my tits." Ric sighed and turned over on his side to face the wall.

"And you lied to the counsellor; if I remember rightly you got Val to break the news to her that we were engaged."

"Shut up, for God's sake."

Arla realised that finding the relief of sleep was going to be elusive, if not downright impossible. Silently fuming with frustration, she switched on her bedside lamp, climbed out of bed, and slipped on her dressing gown.

"I'm going to make a cup of tea. Do you want one?" She looked back at the shape under the bedclothes.

"No."

She let the bedroom door slam to dissipate some of her anger. Stomping downstairs she went into the kitchen and flicked on the light, blinking as the harsh fluorescent bulb spluttered into life. The kettle was still warm from earlier in the evening, and Arla, barefoot on the cold lino, cupped her hands around it, grateful for the single source of heat.

"I've changed my mind. I'll have a cup if you're making one." With a towelling robe around him and rubbing his eyes, Ric padded noiselessly into the kitchen.

"Coffee or tea?"

"Tea please."

She took another cup out of the cupboard.

"This is like old times; me and you in the kitchen at midnight seeing to the kids or making up bottles. Remember?" She looked at him and tried to smile as she brought the memories to mind.

"Yeah; what a nightmare. Awake all night and knackered all day. Shelley hardly slept a wink did she?" He yawned, pulled out a chair from under the table, and sat down.

"Sleep deprivation; a good form of torture, although I'm not sure why we were being punished." Arla gave a wry chuckle as she poured boiling water onto two teabags. "And then Stuart came along."

"I used to go to work and have a kip in the van for an hour first." Ric shook his head at the flood of memories: "I couldn't wait to get out of the house; that hour was all mine."

"I didn't know that!" Arla looked astonished. "I hardly even got five minutes, let alone an hour's sleep!"

"I know, and sometimes I felt guilty, but I knew that if I didn't grab that hour I might have made mistakes at work or drove the van into a wall."

"Now we've got all the time in the world to sleep, and we're still awake." She took the teabags out and added some milk to the cups.

"Different problems now." He took a cup from her outstretched hand.

She sat down opposite him at the kitchen table.

"It scares me sometimes that this problem we have with your mother has come between us like this. I know I've said this before, but it also makes me wonder whether you've been doing the same thing to me all these years." She sipped her tea and looked across at him.

"Doing what?"

"Telling me what you think I want to hear."

"Of course not; don't be daft." He took a gulp of tea but failed to meet her eyes.

"How come we never argue?"

"We do; that's why we're going to the counsellor isn't it?" He shrugged and drained the rest of his cup.

"We only argue about the same subject over and over again. You put Edna before me in everything; it's why I feel the way I do. I've always felt second best to your mother." Arla sighed as she tried to maintain eye contact.

"You're not second best; I love you. I've always put you and the kids first." He put his empty cup down on the table with some force.

"What about the way she treated Shelley and Stuart?" Arla played her trump card with a modicum of finesse. "What are you going on about?" He *tutted* with annoyance.

"You know what I'm talking about; you can't deny that she favourited Shelley over Stuart, and all those years you never pulled her up over it, although I suppose you're going to say it was my fault for letting her interfere too much when Shelley was born." She shook her head and tried to keep the bitterness out of her voice. "The trouble is, you'd never let me say anything to her about staying away and letting me get on with it. When the kids were growing up, if it hadn't been for me trying to hide the fact that your mother preferred Shelley, Stuart might have had a hang-up about it."

Rick kept his eyes focused on the empty cup:

"Well he hasn't got any hang-ups, has he? He's never said anything to me."

"He often did to me though." Arla nodded slightly. "He used to ask why Granny Deane didn't love him, and why it was only Shelley who got the sleepovers."

"Why didn't you tell me that?" He looked up at her quizzically.

"I knew it wouldn't make any difference I suppose." She shrugged.

"You should have told me." Ric stood up. "How could I have done anything about it if you kept things from me?"

Arla collected the cups, stood up, and walked over to put them in the sink.

"That's the whole point; I knew you'd never confront her about it. I had to pretend the problem didn't exist."

"Jesus Christ; I'm not that much of a bastard that I'd let one of my kids go short."

"Well, it's good that I can mention it now, I suppose." Arla turned out the kitchen light. "Come on, let's go back to bed; it's late."

Should she make a move and snuggle up? Arla lay on her side looking at her husband's vast expanse of back close to her face. It was as though by turning away from her Ric was conveying an untold, tacit message. Arla was well aware that Ric was trying to shut her out, and she felt guilty knowing that he was feeling uncomfortable at being made to talk about emotions and situations he would rather have kept hidden.

She reached out an arm and sneaked it around his waist.

"Night night; love you."

There was no reply. Arla was uncertain as to whether Ric was purposely ignoring her or had actually fallen asleep. When the first gentle snore occurred, she sighed, turned over, and prepared for a long night ahead.

CHAPTER 7

IT WAS ONLY after the first few sleepless nights that Arla realised a week's stay on the maternity ward had lulled her into a false sense of security. Her daughter's erratic sleep/wake cycle had become evident from day one; the baby screamed night and day, and Arla was already at the end of her rope. Her mother was not due to retire for another two years, and reluctantly she had had to wave Ric off to work on that first morning. Therefore when the phone rang three days later she picked up the receiver absent-mindedly, too tired to care who the caller was.

"Hello." She yawned.

"This is Edna."

Her heart sank. She knew there was no way her mother-in-law wanted to speak to her. She wished she had not answered the phone at all.

"Oh; Ric's at work I'm afraid."

"Well, actually it's you I was after; I was wondering if I could come round and see the baby."

"I'm a bit tired at the moment; it's not a good time." Arla wished her mother-in-law would hang up and go away.

"I could take Shelley out in the pram for a walk and let you get some sleep if you like."

The offer was too good to turn down. Within an hour she was gratefully handing over her precious bundle to her mother-in-law and sinking unconscious into a soft feathered pillow, her throbbing head already easing with the sudden relief of stress. She slept the deep slumber of the dead until her daughter's hungry cry brought her to sudden reality some two hours later.

"You didn't need to come down; I was just warming up one of the bottles in the fridge for her." Edna rocked the baby expertly with one arm, and checked the temperature of a bottle of milk standing in a saucepan of hot water with the other.

"It's okay, I'll take her now." Arla felt a hot surge of jealousy at the thought of her daughter lying contentedly in the arms of another woman. "Thanks very much for your help." She lifted the baby from Edna's vice-like grip.

"I'll be able to come round every day to give you a hand; I know what it's like when you've just had a baby. I'm surprised you're still not wearing your pyjamas; I was at this stage." Edna chuckled and eyed her granddaughter avidly.

"You don't need to come round every day; I'm sure I'll be fine for a couple of days now I've had some sleep." Arla was aghast at the thought of her mother-in-law taking over her duties.

"Nonsense! Every new mother needs some regular shut-eye. I'll catch the ten thirty bus tomorrow morning; I'll be here by eleven, and then Shelley and I can have a walk out to feed the ducks."

With a faint feeling of foreboding Arla waved Edna off down the garden path and closed the front door with a sigh. When

Ric returned home that evening she was more alert, although clearly worried.

"Ric, your mother has been here today." She kissed him and rocked her daughter back and forth in her arms.

"I wondered when she'd turn up." Ric chuckled. "There's nothing she likes more than cuddling a new-born baby." He gave her a peck on the cheek, and then bent down to kiss Shelley's forehead as she slept.

"Yes, but she's coming back tomorrow, and from what I can gather will probably turn up every single day from now on if I let her."

"What's wrong with that? At least you can get some sleep during the day and get some odd jobs done." Ric shrugged, clearly perplexed.

"Can you have a word with her please, and ask her to just come round twice a week instead?" She looked at him pleadingly.

"No; leave it. You need the help, and she needs something to do. Val and Jan's kids are at school now; she always helped out with them. Let her lend a hand; you never know, you two might become a bit closer."

Appalled at her husband's reply, Arla felt close to tears:

"I don't want her round here every day interfering! Please.....I'm asking you to say something to her; if you don't, then I will."

"It's not worth rocking the boat. Let her take the baby out for a walk, you get some sleep, and then she'll get the bus back home. I can't see what's wrong with that." His tone had become slightly agitated as he hung up his coat.

"Why are you not backing me up?" A tear fell onto her daughter's forehead, who woke up, opened her mouth, and started to yell.

"Look; I've just come in from work. I've had a shit day, and don't need all this as soon as I step through the door." He pushed past her into the kitchen. "What's for dinner?"

She wondered if the hormone upheaval of childbirth was making her overly-melodramatic. Would most new mothers welcome another woman constantly in and out of their house telling them how to bring up their child? Arla thought not, but decided to go along with Ric's reasoning.

"Sorry you've had a bad day; I've made chicken and pasta." She gave him a thin smile whilst soothing the baby, who still smelt faintly of Edna's perfume.

The crunch came when Shelley was fourteen months old. Edna had rushed to pick up Shelley, who had toddled about and fallen over. When Arla saw her daughter hold out her arms to Edna and say '*Mummy*', she knew that enough was enough. She started to make a point of always being out at a different playgroup when she knew that Edna was on her way, and slowly but surely her mother-in-law picked up on the message, although nothing was ever said. However, Arla knew that Edna's sudden separation from her granddaughter, although doing wonders for Shelley's relationship with her rightful mother, had driven a further wedge in the ill-fated mother-in-law/daughter-in-law alliance.

She thought that Ric might possibly mention the fact that his mother was coming to the house less frequently, but to her surprise nothing more was ever said. Arla had prepared her answer, but had decided that she would not be the one to bring the subject up. However, with no more discussion, in time the knotty problem of Edna's absence became relegated to the back burner, leaving Arla to get on with the enjoyable job of bringing up Shelley unencumbered.

CHAPTER 8

"COME TO GRANNY!"

As Edna's arms closed around a delighted Shelley, Arla stood at the bottom of the stairs and looked up.

"Stuart; Granny's here! Come and say hello!" Six-year-old Stuart appeared on the upstairs landing, and with a sigh started to descend the stairs.

"Hello Granny."

Arla noticed that her son's voice seemed devoid of any emotion. Edna had already followed Shelley into the front room, and Stuart's words were lost:

"Shelley's showing Granny her new doll I expect. Hurry along and say hello." Arla kept her voice artificially bright.

"Do I have to?" Stuart whispered conspiratorially up at her.

"It's called being polite." Arla chided gently.

"Okay."

She heard Stuart sigh as he walked slowly behind her to the front room, where she could see Shelley already seated on Edna's lap. Arla smiled.

"I see Shelley's grabbed you already." She gave Stuart a nudge.

"Hello Granny." Stuart smiled.

"Hello. Have you been a good boy?" Edna looked at Shelley and gave her a squeeze. "How's Granny's favourite girl been then?"

Arla was aware that Stuart, politeness forgotten, had slipped quietly out of the room to join his father in the garden.

"Dinner will be at half past twelve as usual." Arla seethed inwardly and purposefully used the shortened version of her husband's name. "I'll let Ric know you're here."

"Where is Richard?"

"Outside."

She found them together, dark heads bent over Stuart's bicycle:

"Your mum's arrived."

"I'll be in when I've put this chain back on." Ric looked up briefly.

"Are you coming in to talk to Granny?" Arla tried one more time to coax her son.

"No, I'm helping Dad."

Her heart melted at the sight of her son, a mini-man at six years old:

"Don't get full of oil and grease; that's a new jumper."

"All right, Mum."

Ensuring her vegetables remained un-sugared and devoid of cheese, Arla took a perverted pleasure in placing a pot of steaming, unadulterated broccoli, carrots and runner beans on the table.

"Not taking any veg, Edna?" She noticed the older woman shaking her head as she passed her the pot.

"No thanks; they're not to my taste."

"Shame. Ric picked the beans from the garden this morning, especially for you." Arla kept a straight face as she looked around at nobody in particular.

"I'll have some roast potatoes though." Edna sniffed. "Could you pass the pot please, Richard?"

"I haven't done roast today; I've done boiled. I forgot to buy oil, and I don't use the fat from the beef." Arla ladled a generous helping of vegetables onto her plate.

"I'll just have the beef and a Yorkshire with some gravy then."

"You sure, Mum?" Ric looked up at his mother with surprise. "No boiled spuds?"

"Not with roast beef; no." Edna sniffed again.

Arla smiled as Stuart laid his knife and fork down on an empty plate:

"What's for pudding, Mum?"

"Well done! Are you going to eat all your dinner today like your brother, Shelley?" She looked at her daughter's miserable face.

"I don't like the broccoli and carrots." Shelley, eight years old, gazed down at her plate.

"I don't blame her. They need some cheese sauce over them. Don't you eat them, darling." Edna looked disdainfully towards the still half-full pot of vegetables.

"I ate mine." Stuart gave his sister a kick under the table.

"How about you, Ric? What's your opinion?" Arla felt a rising anger, and wished she could tip the remainder of the pot over her mother-in-law's head.

"I don't mind either way really. If I'm hungry enough I'll eat anything."

As she watched her husband finishing off the leftovers with gusto, she wanted to run out into the garden, open her mouth, and scream.

"You could have backed me up at dinner, and said the vegetables were lovely."

Arla lay on her back like a wooden statue in the bed, fuming and unforgiving. Ric, distant and cold, turned his face to the wall away from her.

"I ate them, didn't I? Surely that's enough?"

"Once, just once disagree with your mother; I dare you." "Don't start on that again."

"Night night." She turned on her side so that their backs were almost touching.

"Yeah; night night."

CHAPTER 9

ARLA IDLY NOTED Toni Beecher opening her notebook to the last page she had written on, before turning her attention to Ric.

"Were you aware of any issues regarding your children and their grandmother?"

"No; not really. I knew Shelley was closer to her granny than Stuart, but I thought that was just because they were both girls and had more in common. Stuart tended to follow me about or be out playing with his mates." Ric shrugged and crossed his legs.

"How do you feel about your wife's revelations?"

"We talked about this a couple of days' ago. If I had known our son felt left out I would have spoken to my mother about it."

"No you wouldn't; that's the whole point. Edna interfered for months when Shelley was born, and you never said a word to her." Arla sighed. "You still wouldn't say anything today."

"Well it's not relevant now, is it? Stuart's twenty three for God's sake!" Ric gave a snort of annoyance.

"It's good that you've both had a talk. Was it the first time you've spoken about some of your issues?" Toni interjected and glanced quickly between them.

"I suppose so; we tried anyway. I also told him I wondered if he's been treating me the same way as his mother all these years." Arla kept her eyes fixed on the counsellor.

"Could you elaborate a bit more on that statement, please?" Toni picked up her pen.

"Well, you know; just saying only what I wanted to hear, and keeping his real thoughts to himself." Arla shrugged and gave a quick sideways look at Ric.

Toni took a sip of water from a glass on the coffee table before continuing:

"For any marriage to work successfully I say to both parties that they need to be absolutely truthful and transparent with one another in their thoughts and feelings. Truth is the cornerstone with which to build foundations that last a lifetime, and with this truth comes trust."

"I trust Ric; I mean, he hasn't had affairs or anything like that. It's the truth bit that I have issues with. I don't think he tells me everything."

"What do you want to know? Have I got to tell you even when I need a shit?" Ric sighed, folded his arms, and crossed his legs.

"No, of course not. It's being able to talk through all our problems, even if we have differences of opinion. It's being able to talk about things in an adult way without you becoming defensive and walking out of the room or ignoring the situation completely."

Toni nodded silently.

"We need to learn how to discuss our problems in a certain way, without becoming argumentative. For instance, Mrs Deane, instead of accusing your husband of something which might instantly put him on the defensive, you could start your conversation by stating how you feel about a particular situation. You've a perfect right to let your husband know how you feel about something, and vice versa of course."

Arla, cut to the quick at Toni's blatant criticism, nodded in agreement:

"Okay. So for instance I could say to Ric that I feel I have been mistreated by his mother and sisters throughout our marriage; one of the reasons being due to the fact that his sisters automatically believe their mother when she tells them lies about something I've apparently said or done."

"Yes; can you see how much better that sounds rather than accusing him of taking his mother's side against you?" Toni nodded to emphasise her point.

"Sure, but it still doesn't get us anywhere." Arla turned sideways to face Ric on the sofa. "His mother and his sisters still hate me, but I don't know why."

"Mr Deane, do you feel you could reply to your wife's statement at this time?" Toni jotted down a few words before looking up from her notepad.

"My answer is the same as it's always been. My mum and my sisters are part of my immediate family, and I don't want to fall out with them. I'm staying neutral on this; Arla knows how I feel about not wanting to upset the status quo." Ric sighed. "I don't know how many more times I have to say the same thing over and over again."

Arla looked again at her husband sitting stiff and unyielding on the sofa, and wondered how she had managed to live with a partner for so many years who offered her not one jot of support.

"What about the phone problem. What about all the lies? I feel I've been victimised since day one."

"What are you talking about now?" Ric exhaled with venom.

"Remember when caller display started to come in and Edna would recognise our phone number? If I had to phone her for something she would pick up and say '*Hello Richard*' without even waiting to hear who was on the other end? I mean….how rude is that?" Arla shook her head. "And surely you can't have forgotten when she rang up last year and wanted her loft cleared out there and then? I picked up the phone when you were at work and said you couldn't help right away because you had a lot of work booked with customers for the rest of the week, but you were free to help all over the weekend. I found out she then phoned your sisters and told her that I'd said you couldn't help her at all. Val gave me a rollicking down the phone, and both of your sisters haven't spoken to me since." Arla's voice trembled with emotion. "You never spoke to your mother about it. It was just left and forgotten about. I'm apparently the bad guy here, but I don't feel as though I've done anything wrong. Nobody ever asked me for my side of the story."

The injustice of the situation hit her again, causing fresh tears to fall down her face. She felt embarrassed to cry in front of a stranger, and attempted to hide her head in her hands.

"I now don't answer the phone at all if I can see it's his mother calling. I feel that if I don't speak to her, then she can't twist my words around when she reports back to his sisters, because everything I say or do gets back to them sooner or later. Ms Beecher, the situation now is that I don't speak to his family at all, but Ric still talks to them as though nothing's happened." She wiped her eyes with a tissue. "I've noticed that now they've all stopped ringing the landline and only call Ric's mobile. I'm being victimised for something else now; I've no idea what, and he won't take my side in this. Sitting here and going over it all again I sometimes feel like I want to move out. What's the point in trying to live with somebody who offers you no moral support?" Her voice came in sobbing hiccoughs as she gave in to her anger and frustration. "There were other times when he could have intervened as well, but never did."

"Would you like to tell me what they were?" Toni looked at Arla with interest.

"Well, for instance; his mother has a big collage of family photos on the wall in her front room." Arla was filled with relief at being able to talk about an issue which had been upsetting her for quite some time. "The only person missing from the collage is myself; there's a photo of Ric on our wedding day, but just Ric and not me. Also she buys Ric Christmas presents and birthday presents, but never me; not that I'm greedy for a present, it's just that for instance I could never buy our daughter a Christmas present without also buying one for our son-in-law. It's rude when your child is married to ignore their spouse, don't you think? Also there were the years when I was a new mother when she would interfere and undermine me in front of my children, especially where food was concerned. However, Ric would never say a word against her."

"Mrs Deane, thank you for sharing your thoughts. I'm now going to ask your husband if he would like to comment." Toni Beecher looked towards Ric. "Mr Deane; have you any answer to your wife's statement?"

With a rising feeling of dread, Arla watched as Ric stood up, walked out of the room, and slammed the front door.

Making her excuses and leaving, she saw him leaning back against the head-rest with his eyes closed as she approached the car door.

"Don't say anything. I don't want to talk about my mother, my sisters, or our relationship. Keep quiet and you'll be doing just fine." Ric started the car's engine and selected first gear.

"Just as long as you don't shoot off like a rocket again and kill us both." Arla sat down in the passenger seat, slammed the car door, and set her lips into a firm line.

"That's the last time I'm going there for your information. The woman's obviously on your side anyway." Ric looked over his shoulder and pulled away from the kerb.

"At least somebody is then." She closed her eyes to shut out her husband and the world.

A deathly silence fell for the rest of the journey, which was only broken by the ringing of the landline as Arla turned the key in the lock.

"Hello!" Breathless on running, she picked up the phone without checking the number.

"Hi Mum!"

"Hello Stuart! Nice to hear from you!"

"I phoned earlier and then tried your mobile. Where have you been?"

"Oh......only out shopping." She lied. "How are you?"

"Great! Never been better actually. Er...can I come for a visit at the weekend?"

"Sure, it'll be lovely to see you. Come for Sunday lunch if you like?"

"Will do. I'll be bringing someone with me if that's okay?"

His voice sounded upbeat and happier than usual. Arla felt a *frisson* of jealousy shoot through her at the only possible reason for her son's bonhomie.

"Have you found a girlfriend then?" She held her breath as she waited for his response.

"Not *a* girl, *the* girl. I've found the one I want to marry. You'll love her Mum, she's adorable!"

"Oh, wow! What's her name?" Arla tried to summon up the correct amount of bonhomie for her new daughter-in-law.

"Ria. She can't wait to meet you! I'm absolutely crazy about her!"

They had only visited Stuart a few times. She thought back to the trendy sushi bars and vegan restaurants near his Edwardian terraced house in Clapham Common.

"Does she like roast chicken? Is she vegetarian?"

"Mum; she eats most things. Don't worry."

"Shall I ask Shelley and Dave as well?"

"We'll meet them another time. Let's just make it us four on Sunday."

"Okay. I'll look forward to it then. Come about mid-day."

"Great! See you then!"

She felt shell-shocked as she replaced the receiver.

"Who was that?" Ric took his coat off and hung it over the bannister.

"Stuart. He's bringing the girl he wants to marry to dinner on Sunday."

"Bloody hell; have we got to play happy families then?"

"For Sunday anyway. Let's try at any rate; you may even get to like it." She sighed as she looked at him.

"I do like it; I want us to be happy. I hate all these arguments. It's pointless; we just go round and round in circles."

"Don't you think that counselling is helping us?" She sat on the stairs, deflated and depressed.

"No, because I'm not going to upset my eighty-year-old mother and dredge up all the family's dirty linen from years ago. Just let it lie; you don't speak to her, and she doesn't speak to you. Leave it like that and for Christ's sake let's forget about it." He stepped past her. "I'm going up to have a shower."

Arla flopped down onto the settee and tried to imagine what sort of girl Stuart would be bringing home to meet them. His career at the bank was going from strength to strength; she supposed they had probably met at work. *Was she a high flyer? How would she react to her future in-laws? Was she hoping for an intellectual discussion with them on stocks and shares and portfolios over the dinner table?* Arla suddenly felt inadequate at the thought of trying to appear erudite and learned. *She and Ric were just ordinary people; she had been a housewife for so long that all she could talk about were recipes and the best type of washing powder. Ric would probably be his usual taciturn self.*

The whole scenario gave her the willies.

CHAPTER 10

"DO YOU HAVE a good relationship with your own children, now that they're adults?" Toni smiled and glanced up at Arla with interest.

"Sure; we get along fine. I've always got on well with my daughter, but I don't see Shelley now as much as I'd like because she and her husband live about an hour's drive away. They're self-employed and busy running their own business." Arla wondered where Toni's train of thought was heading.

"What about your son?"

"He lives down in London. I must admit there were a few differences of opinion as he was growing up." Arla exhaled and looked at the empty seat next to her on the sofa.

"Such as?"

"Oh; the usual teenage tantrums. For instance; he wanted to sleep on the beach for the weekend with a group of friends when he was about fourteen. We said no." "And how did he take that?" Toni chuckled.

"He sneaked out and did it anyway. We grounded him for a month." Arla recalled with a shudder her son's four week campaign of door-slamming, sulking, and non-cooperation.

"So he was more headstrong than your daughter?"

"Oh yes; absolutely. We even had the police round as well, when he was about fifteen." Arla rolled her eyes to the ceiling.

"What for?" Toni suppressed a smile.

"He'd got hold of a friend's air rifle and shot a hole in somebody's front door who we didn't know, but who lived further down the road from us. The chap in question called the police and my son received a caution, but as far as Stuart was concerned the man had it coming as he'd exposed himself to the mother of one of his friends." Arla gave a wry smile at her then teenage son's warped logic.

"So, I think we can safely say that the relationship with your son as he was growing up did not mirror the type experienced by your husband and his mother?" Toni shook her head.

"Definitely; Stuart has always been his own man. If he didn't agree with something we'd done or said, then he would have let us know about it." Arla nodded to confirm her statement. "Quite a lot of the time he'd go on to do exactly the opposite of what we'd asked of him in the first place."

"A typical teenager then!" Toni chuckled once more.

"Oh yes. That's why I can't understand Ric's pandering to his mother's every whim. It doesn't seem like a normal relationship to me." Arla shrugged. "Stuart was never like that."

"And how about now?" Toni questioned Arla gently. "Is there still the odd difference of opinion?"

"Sometimes, but nothing to worry about. Stuart's an adult; of course he's going to think differently from me from time to time. I'd worry if he *didn't* have his own opinions."

Toni finished writing and then turned over the page.

"How do you get on with your children's partners?"

"Shelley's husband Dave is a decent chap; hard-working and likeable. You can have a laugh with him. Stuart's fiancée I've yet to meet; he's bringing her home to meet us at the weekend." Arla kept her face expressionless.

"How does your son's engagement make you feel?" Toni smiled enigmatically.

"I think he's too young to settle down, but as I said before, Stuart will do whatever he wants." Arla shrugged.

"Does it anger you when your son doesn't listen to your suggestions?" Toni tapped her pen against the side of her notebook.

"Sometimes, but I'm quite used to it; he never did take any notice of me anyway." Arla sighed whilst trying to conjure up a picture of Stuart's fiancée in her mind.

"Would you rather he just agreed with everything you suggest?" The twinkle in Toni's eye was evident.

"Oh, no; not really. I mean…. How warped would that be?" Arla shook her head.

CHAPTER 11

DISTURBING ONE OF the net curtain's symmetrical pleats with one hand and smoothing back her recently dyed hair with the other, she took a quick peep at Ria as her future daughter-in-law stepped out of the car. She noticed the girl's shiny nut-brown bob, as the wind whipped it around her face.

"She's quite a big girl. I thought Stuart always liked them skinny."

She let the curtain fall again and turned away from the window, feeling a stab of envy on noticing her son giving his new fiancée a look of adoration as they walked up the driveway hand in hand. In a split second she remembered the first years of her own marriage, and how an extremely satisfying session of cunnilingus could cause her to smile at Ric in exactly the same way. She sighed; her son was lost to her now, and she was no longer the most important person in his life.

Ric folded his Sunday newspaper and pushed it down the side of his armchair.

"At least she won't be pushing a lettuce leaf around the plate then, like that other one he brought home before."

"Her top is too low. Try not to stare at her chest when you meet her." Arla's lips registered a pout of disapproval.

"I'll do my best. I'll talk to her but if you like I'll look up at the ceiling at the same time; I'm sure she won't notice anything amiss." Ric shrugged and got to his feet.

"You know what I mean. All the girls wear low scoop necks these days; it does nothing for the imagination. Why can't they cover up and have a bit of decorum?" Arla sighed again and followed Ric towards the front door.

"What's wrong with showing a bit of titty?" Ric looked back over his shoulder at her and chuckled. "There's worse things to look at."

"No there's not." Arla shook her head. "I don't want someone's heaving cleavage right in my face."

"It's handy if you're looking for somewhere to park your bike." Ric kept a straight face as he turned the handle.

"Don't be sexist." Arla's face registered disapproval, but with the hint of a smile.

"Hi Mum! Hi Dad!" Stuart grinned. "Meet Ria, the love of my life!" Still holding his fiancée's hand, he stepped into the hallway.

"Hello Ria; pleased to meet you." Arla held out her hand.

"How's it going Ria?" Ric's eyes automatically strayed southwards.

"Hi. What do I call you both?" Ria smiled, and with her left hand still holding Stuart's, she clasped Arla's hand with her own.

"Arla is fine, and Stuart's dad likes to be called Ric."

"Okay. Do you still call Stuart by his full name then? Everyone in London calls him Stu." Ria turned to Ric. "Hi. How are you?"

"I'm fine thanks." Ric managed to tear his eyes away from Ria's substantial chest just in time.

"We've always called him Stuart." Arla sniffed. "Otherwise he'd surely sound like a casserole."

"It doesn't matter, Mum; I've been called a lot worse. Come and have a cuddle. What's for dinner?"

Arla found herself enveloped in a bear hug, all the while noticing that Ria had stood awkwardly to one side.

"Mmm, you smell lovely. What's the aftershave?"

"Ria bought it for me. She likes it, but I can't remember what it's called."

Looking out from the comfort of her son's arms, she wanted the moment to last forever.

"I hope you both like roast chicken with all the trimmings." She kissed Stuart on the cheek, and noticed with a start that his dark blond hair was already beginning to recede at the temples.

"You know I do!" Stuart picked her up and swung her round.

"Put me down! Ria, do you like Sunday roast?" Arla giggled as she disentangled herself from Stuart's embrace.

"I'll eat the chicken and roast potatoes, but I don't like vegetables much; peas and carrots maybe, but nothing else. Sorry." Ria looked to her fiancé for encouragement.

"Ria was never made to eat any vegetables. I'm introducing her to them slowly." Stuart bounded over to Ria and folded a protective arm about her shoulder.

"Looks like it'll be chicken, Yorkshire and spuds then Ria?" Arla shrugged but secretly longed for another bear hug.

"That's fine." Ria's face took on a martyred look.

"I've cooked the roast potatoes with olive oil by the way. I know it's different from most people, but that's how we like it." Arla held her breath in anticipation.

"Oh? My mum always told me to use the fat from the meat." Ria replied confidently.

"Come in and sit down at the table; Mum was just about to dish up. I'll get the drinks in." Ric ushered his guests into the dining room.

"Dad; Ria just has soft drinks for now." Stuart grinned at his fiancée as he followed behind his father.

"No wine?" Ric looked from Stuart to Ria, and then back again.

"Not at the moment." Ria's smile was fixed.

"Drying out are you, girl?" Ric chuckled. "Is it the morning after the night before?"

"Well, there's something we want to tell you, but we'll wait until Mum comes in."

Stuart pulled out a dining chair for Ria, and then seated himself next to her. Ric took another approving glance at his new daughter-in-law's chest as she sat down.

"Here it is; Ric, where's the wine?" Arla wheeled in steaming pots and a platter of meat on a hostess trolley.

"No wine for Ria, Mum. We've just found out that she's pregnant. We wanted to tell you both as soon as we knew." Stuart gazed at Ria with doe-like eyes.

"Congratulations son!" Ric hid his surprise well, and clapped Stuart on the back. "This calls for some champagne, but wine will have to do because we haven't got any!"

"Oh, my goodness, it makes me feel old!" Arla did not know whether to laugh or cry. "Stuart, we had no idea!"

"Neither did we until a few days ago. Your first grandchild is due on the twentieth of October." Stuart grinned. "We're very happy."

"Are you earning enough?" Will you still be able to pay your mortgage?"

"Don't worry Mum; the bank have promoted me to Supervisor. That was our other bit of news."

"Oh, well done! I just *know* you'll be manager there one day. All that studying is starting to pay off now."

Arla tried not to let a small sigh of frustration escape from her lips for her son's weakness at the initial sight of two wobbling mammary glands of, as far as she could covertly tell, approximate cup size 40DD.

"I hope so. Ria's soon going to give up her job at the supermarket, as she's often feeling sick and tired now, so we're going to need the extra money." Stuart nuzzled his nose against Ria's, who gave him another knowing look.

"Help yourself to whatever you want, Ria. You're eating for two now." Ric smiled and uncovered the vegetable pots.

"Thanks; I'll have some chicken and some roast potatoes and peas, please." Ria added some slices of chicken to her plate. "Sorry, but I don't do cauliflower or red cabbage."

"Just eat what you want. We're very happy to have you here, aren't we Arla?" Ric nodded in Arla's direction.

"Of course; we're absolutely delighted."

Arla, slightly relieved at now not needing any knowledge of stocks and shares, hoped she had mustered up just the right amount of enthusiasm to sound genuinely thrilled at the news, but later on the pseudo-smile faltered just as soon as her son's car pulled off the driveway.

"She's dense! She's using Stuart as a gravy train! He's only twenty three; what does he want to get bogged down with babies for at his age?"

"That sounds similar to what your dad said to you at our engagement party."

Ric's statement infuriated Arla even more, and she paced up and down the front room in anger.

"Good God; he said they only met six months ago! All she had to do was flash her tits, open her legs, and there you have it; job jobbed!"

Ric read the same sentence twice more before giving up and flinging his newspaper on the floor.

"For God's sake calm down! He's happy; can't you see?"

"He's still a boy! He should be out with his mates getting pissed, not fawning over that girl." She flopped down onto the settee. "He'll have no money now he's got to keep three of them. His brain's gone soft with sex. You can see she's as thick as two short planks. She'll be no asset to him at all." She sighed in exasperation.

"He's a man now; he makes his own decisions." Ric shrugged. "He didn't seem too unhappy about becoming a father; quite the reverse in fact."

"That's because he doesn't realise what pressure he's going to be under to keep the bills paid and the food on the table. I wanted more for our son. Not only his job, what about his drums and the band and the weekend gigs? He's not going to have time for that either once the baby comes along." Arla wanted to scream at her son for his stupidity.

"I expect he knows that. We can't dictate to him how to live his life." Ric crossed his legs. "I willingly sold my motorbike when Shelley was born. Remember?"

"That's not the same thing." She sighed, unconvinced.

"Of course it is! We needed the money, and the bike was impractical. It belonged to my bachelor days, and I'd become a responsible husband and father."

"And your mother wanted you to spend the money on more courses to further your education, but we used it to put a deposit down on a flat." Arla closed her eyes and rested her head on the back of the settee.

"Don't you see what I mean? I was happy to sell my bike and make a home for us. And do you have to bring my mother into every single conversation?"

"Well, Stuart won't be happy giving up the band; I know that." Arla, eyes still shut, ignored her husband's last statement.

"That's where you're wrong. You've got it all arse about tit." Ric shook his head. "Oops no, I mustn't mention tits must I?"

Arla stood up again, brown eyes blazing.

"You like the girl, don't you? I could see your eyes straying to her chest. She's got you sucked in as well, hasn't she? I bet she's got no qualifications. All she does is work in a supermarket. Can't you see she's cottoned on to our son for an easy life?"

"A bloke can't help but notice if a girl's got large bazoomas, but it doesn't mean anything. I've got nothing against her. As far as I'm concerned she's having our grandchild, and our son loves her. It's good enough for me and it's going to have to be good enough for you, otherwise your anger is going to eat you up inside." Ric picked up his newspaper. "End of subject. Over and out."

CHAPTER 12

"HELLO TONI; CAN I call you Toni? I feel as if I know you a bit better now; and do call me Arla if you like." Arla settled herself on the sofa and poured herself a glass of water from a jug on the coffee table. She was getting used to the sight of the cluttered bookshelves, heavy draperies, and cloying aroma of joss sticks.

"Of course; I prefer first name terms too. Is your husband not joining us again today?" Toni Beecher indicated towards the empty space on the sofa.

"I tried to get him to change his mind, but he's not coming back."

Toni Beecher sifted back through her notes and took a quick glance at her watch at the same time.

"That's a shame. Have you and your husband managed to talk a little bit more about your problems?"

Arla shook her head:

"It's no good; he's not going to budge. We've reached impasse. I don't even know if I like living with him anymore. I still don't feel as though he's on my side, or will ever be, come to think of it."

"It's quite normal to feel anger against a partner whom you feel is not giving you any support, but I would like to ask you a couple of questions if I may." Toni played with her pen.

"What questions?" Arla looked at Toni inquisitively.

"Number one; do you love your husband, and number two; if the love is still there, at some point in the future do you think you can forgive him for his impartiality?" Toni cocked her head to one side and waited for an answer.

The clock ticked loudly in the silence of the room. Arla sighed and sniffed.

"I do love him, but we're not the same people that we were twenty eight years ago."

"Who is? We all grow and change with time." Toni nodded slightly to emphasise her point. "Our views and opinions alter with maturity. It's a natural progression."

"Yes I agree, but when I married Ric I thought it would be us against the world. It's never been that way though unfortunately. I *know* I come second to his mother." Arla played with a strand of hair.

"Do you think your husband's opinion has changed over the years regarding his mother?" Toni jotted down a few more notes.

"No; it's stayed the same."

"So can we say that in effect, you were aware of how your husband felt about his mother when you married him?" Toni lifted her head from her notebook for eye contact.

Arla felt uncomfortable with the way the conversation was progressing:

"I found it strange that they never argued. My mum and I used to shout at each other like a pair of old fishwives when I was a teenager, and Stuart and I have had a few ding-dongs, but I didn't know the extent of Ric's sycophancy until we'd been married a few years."

"I see. Do you think your husband will ever change his outlook at all regarding his mother?" Toni's pen poised perfectly over a blank page.

"No; it's hopeless." Arla's eyes filled with tears of frustration.

"So, moving on from my original two questions, do you think you may eventually be able to accept that your husband will probably always remain of a neutral opinion in any argument between his mother and yourself?"

"Well, by talking to you I realise that unless I divorce him I've no choice *but* to accept it, have I?" Arla sighed and folded her arms. "Anyway…what's new? I've been accepting it for twenty eight years."

"We all have choices, and we must choose wisely." Toni looked at Arla. "Have you thought about what choices you must make to resolve your problems?"

A wry smile appeared on Arla's lips.

"There are no choices, and I know I'll have to put up with being second place. I am nearly fifty years old. My chance to further my nursing career has long gone while I was at home raising children, and as I have no income of my own I have no choice but to stay with my husband."

"So you feel that any choice you might make is out of your control?" Toni looked quizzically at Arla.

"Absolutely. I have no control over anything, do I?" Arla shrugged.

"Is it important that you feel you are in control of a situation?" Toni jotted notes down frantically.

"Yes it's important, because I'm not in control and I want to be I suppose." Arla sighed."

"In control of ………..*what* exactly?" Toni looked up briefly from her notebook.

"My life; I can't get what I want."

"And what is that?"

"To be number one in Ric's life." Arla exhaled forcefully with irritation. "Can't you see what I'm getting at?"

"But Ric's choice is to stay neutral. However, this doesn't necessarily mean that you aren't important to him though." Toni's voice was calm. "Do you feel it is appropriate to be in control of somebody else's choices?"

"No…..but…" Arla floundered on unfamiliar territory.

"We've a perfect right to feel in control of our own choices in life, but problems begin if we try to exert control over somebody else's." Toni nodded energetically. "Do you understand?"

"Only too clearly." Arla kept her arms folded and crossed her legs. "You've now more or less told me that I'm trying to control Ric."

"And are you? How would you answer that?" Toni smiled and put down her pen.

"I'd say I want to go away now and think about all of this."

Arla, embarrassed and emotionally drained, fished in her handbag, drew forty pounds from her purse, and stood up.

"Thanks for listening. Can I come back next week?" "Of course; I'll be here for as long as you need me."
Toni smiled and extended her arm towards Arla.

"Goodbye for now." Arla clasped Toni's right hand with her own.

"Goodbye."

CHAPTER 13

SHE RECOGNISED THE number as soon as she saw it flashing on the caller display screen.

"Hi Jan."

"Is Richard there please?"

Arla heard the familiar clipped tones and gritted her teeth.

"Ric's at work at the moment. Can I take a message?"

"No thanks. I've tried him on his mobile, but there's no answer."

"He probably hasn't got any signal." Arla made a fist of her right hand, palm upwards, and raised her middle finger towards the phone.

"I'll try him again later then." The phone went dead.

Still looking at the phone, Arla replaced the receiver, added a raised middle finger of her left hand for good measure, and moved both digits up and down alternately.

"Bitch!"

The counselling session would now probably make dinner late. Peeling and chopping root vegetables with gusto, Arla boiled some skinless turkey pieces in a saucepan, adding in some herby stock and corn-flour. After tipping in some lentils with the sliced carrots, onions and parsnips, she peeled some mushrooms and stirred them into the casserole. Satisfied to see the concoction simmering away, she made herself a cup of tea and sat down to read the newspaper.

The phone rang again.

Sighing at the sight of the caller display panel, she picked up the phone:

"Hi Val."

"Where's Richard?"

"Ric's at work with probably no phone signal. Do you want to leave a message?"

"Just tell him to ring me when he comes in."

The dialling tone returned before she had a chance to reply. Arla screamed to nobody in particular, gave the casserole a hearty stir, and settled down again to read. When she heard Ric's key turn in the lock after about an hour she jumped up and went out into the hallway.

"Something smells nice." He kissed her perfunctorily on the cheek.

"It's a turkey casserole, but it's not quite ready yet because I went along for more counselling."

"Oh? How'd it go?"

"It's all my fault. I'm trying to control you."

"What a load of bollocks." Ric hung his coat up on a hook. "You're wasting your money."

"I don't think so. Toni says she'll be happy to see me again."

"I bet she will; at forty quid a go she'll be hanging on in there until they carry her out in a coffin."

"Did your sisters get you on the phone?" She ignored his remark and gave him a hug.

"No. I didn't have any signal this afternoon. What did they want?"

"They wouldn't tell me."

"I'll give Val a ring then."

She followed behind him into the kitchen, and sat down to complete the crossword as Ric picked up the landline phone. As he began to speak she realised from the tone of his voice that something was wrong, and waited impatiently for him to finish the conversation whilst idly answering a few easy questions. When at length he replaced the receiver, she put down her pen and looked up at him.

"What's up?" She noticed his serious expression.

"It's Mum; she's been taken to hospital. Val found her in agony with chest pains; she thinks it might be a heart attack."

"Oh." She stood up. "Why on earth wouldn't they tell me what was wrong? I could have let you know as soon as you came in."

"Never mind; it's okay; I'll go up to the hospital after dinner and find out what's happened. Are you coming with me?"

He sat down wearily at the kitchen table and sought her eyes with his own. Arla hadn't the heart to refuse him.

"Yes, if you want me to." She shrugged. "Although I don't expect your mother will be particularly over the moon to see me at her sickbed."

"You're part of the family. Where I go, you go; she'll have to get used to it." Ric smiled. "Thanks for agreeing to come along."

"My pleasure, I think." She chuckled and stood up. "I'll just check if the casserole's ready."

CHAPTER 14

THE UNPLEASANT AROMA of yesterday's boiled cabbage coupled with more than a faint essence of faces hit her as she opened the main door to the Westen hospital's cardiac ward.

"Could you tell me whereabouts Edna Deane is please?" Arla spoke to a rather harassed young healthcare assistant.

"Second bay; third bed on the left."

"Thanks."

She followed behind Ric, wanting to make herself as inconspicuous as possible. On entering bay 2 she saw both Val and Jan were already there; two vituperous vultures each trying to outdo the other as they fussed around Edna, who held court in pseudo-regal splendour.

"Richard! How lovely to see you!" Edna smiled and held out her arms.

"Hi Mum! What's been going on then?" Ric gave his mother a kiss, and sat down next to her on the bed.

"Hello Edna". Arla's face registered a fixed smile.

Edna hugged her son, but did not return her daughter-in-law's greeting. Arla ignored the snub, smiled maniacally at her mother-in-law, and silently seated herself in an empty chair at the end of the bed.

"I've got a blocked artery, Richard; they're going to put a stent in."

"Mum's staying in for a few days until she's had it done, then she's got to take it easy." Val plumped up the pillows behind Edna's head.

"No more rushing around for you now." Jan *tutted,* shook her head, and poured Edna some more water.

"If you need anything, just let me know." Ric patted Edna's hand.

"I have such wonderful children. Whatever would I do without you?" Edna smiled and lay back weakly on the pillows.

From her island in the middle of the ward, Arla supposed that Edna's sweet tooth had finally caught up with her. She could also not help but notice that neither Val, Jan nor Edna had even once glanced in her direction. She felt awkward and wanted to be gone, yet desired at least a cursory acknowledgement of her presence. Nerves caused her to blurt out the first thing that came into her head.

"No more cream cakes for you then, Edna."

She likened the next scene to a cold frost descending its icy tentacles far and wide. Val, groomed to perfection even on a hospital ward, fired off the first retort in an angry, clipped tone.

"Mum will eat just what she wants to eat." Val sniffed and kept her eyes on Edna.

"If she wants a cream cake, then she shall have one." Jan, her back turned towards Arla, pulled up the bedclothes to cover Edna's chest.

"I don't need anybody telling me how to manage my life, thanks." Edna smiled at her daughters and threw a knowing look in their direction.

"Then you'll probably end up with two stents instead of one." Arla stood up and looked at Ric. "I'll be waiting outside when you're done."

With her head held high, Arla walked past several pairs of rheumy eyes to the exit. Happy to be away from the ward and sighing with relief on finding herself in a cool, empty corridor, she walked quickly until she found herself outside in the fresh air. Realising that Ric still had the car keys, she waited in a queue for the bus alongside several mournful hospital visitors, and sent a text to let him know she was safely on board.

The bus wended its slow, convoluted way around the back streets of Westen, picking up and depositing its human cargo. Arla screamed silently at the length of the journey, which would have taken a quarter of the time in Ric's car. Arriving at the end of her street, she jumped off just in time to see Ric's car overtaking the bus. By the time she made it home she could see that he had pulled the curtains and switched on the porch light.

"Why didn't you wait?" He came out into the hallway to greet her.

"You heard how they spoke to me. I couldn't get away fast enough." She threw down her bag. "That's the last time I'm ever going anywhere near your mother and sisters. I've never felt so humiliated!" She ripped off her coat and dumped it on top of her bag.

"Sorry; that was my fault. I shouldn't have asked you to come." He moved closer and gave her a hug.

"I wanted to go to support you, but I was nervous and said the first thing that came into my head." Arla sighed and enjoyed the feel of her cheek against his chest.

Ric chuckled and slid his arms around her back.

"The old girl could definitely do with eating a few less cream cakes, that's for sure!"

"I know; I was just trying to help." Arla looked up at him. "Perhaps she doesn't know her diet's killing her?"

"Oh, she knows all right, but she's too old to change her ways now." He shrugged and moved towards the kitchen, keeping one arm around her shoulders. "Come on; I'll make you a cup of tea."

The phone rang as he switched the kettle on to boil. Lifting the receiver Arla smiled as she recognised the number:

"Hello Stuart!"

"It's Ria."

"Oh; sorry."

"I was just ringing to find out how Edna is. Val spoke to Stu earlier."

"She's got a blocked artery, but she'll be okay once she's had a stent fitted." She inwardly winced at the abbreviation to her son's name. "How are you?"

"I'm definitely getting a little bump now."

"That's great." Arla tried to hide her disappointment that the caller was not Stuart.

"Er.......would you and Ric like to come to dinner next Sunday?" Ria's voice sounded young and upbeat. "Shelley and Dave are coming too."

"Oh, yes, that'll be great, thanks." Arla looked over at Ric. "See you on Sunday then. Do you want me to bring anything?"

"No; just yourselves."

"Was that Stuart?" Ric poured boiling water into two cups and added a teabag to each.

"No; Ria."

"Why did you think it was Stuart then?" He added some milk and took out the teabags.

"I don't know. I just assumed it was. It always was for ages when he was there on his own."

"Not any more he's not; he lives with Ria now. You moan that my mum always assumes it's me when you phone, but now you're doing the same."

"At least I'll have a photo of *both* of them on their wedding day on our mantelpiece, not just Stuart, and Ria will even get Christmas and birthday presents as well." Arla bridled with years of pent-up resentment. "And you never know, I might even invite her for a girly spa weekend or a few days away to make up for all the times your mother and sisters never invited me on theirs."

"Don't start that old gramophone record up again." Ric sighed and stirred both cups with a spoon.

"Why do Edna and your sisters always cut me out of everything? It's so rude!"

"I don't know, is the answer to that."

"Why won't you do anything about it?"

"It's not worth it."

"It is to me."

"Just give it a rest. It won't do any good in the long run."

He picked up a cup of tea and handed it to her. She felt like throwing it in his face.

CHAPTER 15

"SHELLEY! I HAVEN'T seen you for weeks!" Arla hugged her daughter. "How are you?"

"I'm fine Mum; we're both fine." Shelley laughed and tossed back her shoulder length auburn hair. "It seems that my little brother has beaten me to parenthood!"

"It was definitely a bit of a shock to be told I'm going to be a grandmother!" Arla grimaced. "I'm still getting used to it."

"How's Granny?" Shelley kissed her mother's cheek. "As

far as I know she's had the stent and is now at home resting." Arla shrugged.

"I'll give her a call." Shelley confirmed her statement with a brief nod.

"How's the shop doing?"

"Great!" Shelley grinned enthusiastically. "We've got so many orders it looks as though we'll be taking somebody else on soon."

"That's good news. I'm so pleased for you." Arla smiled.

She followed Shelley into Stuart and Ria's main living area and looked around at the sparse furnishings. The

Edwardian terrace had received several makeovers by previous owners in the past, and currently sported trendy whitewashed walls, white enamel radiators, spotlights on the ceilings, and some pot pourri in the now defunct fireplace. She nudged Shelley and whispered conspiratorially out of earshot of Ria.

"There's not much furniture, is there?"

"Perhaps they don't have a lot of money." Shelley shrugged and looked around. "Although this is London isn't it? Perhaps less is more?"

They were giggling together as Ria came in from the kitchen carrying a tray.

"Drinks are served. Where are the boys?"

"They're out looking at Stuart's new car." Shelley rolled her eyes. "Dave hasn't even been in here yet; Stuart grabbed him in the hallway."

"Dad's out there too now. Can we help you with dinner at all, Ria?" Arla glanced at Ria questioningly.

"No; it's okay. We don't usually have a roast on Sundays, so I'm doing pizza and pasta." Ria placed a jug of Pimms and lemonade down on the table. "Help yourselves; it'll be lunch on your laps though because we don't have a table big enough."

Arla exchanged a glance with Shelley, and whispered after Ria had left the room:

"Pizza on my lap for Sunday lunch?" She wrinkled her nose.

"Looks like it." Shelley chuckled. "You didn't complain when you ate burgers at ours when we first moved in."

"At least you had a table to put them on."

"We are getting a table, but the mortgage and having to buy baby things are taking our money at the moment." Ria came back into the room noiselessly with a second tray of soft drinks. "I hope you understand."

"So sorry." Arla blushed. "I didn't mean to sound rude; I was just joking with Shelley."

"That's okay." Ria's face registered no emotion. "I'll call the boys in for lunch."

The pizza was steaming and the pasta had been tossed in a tasty garlic sauce. Arla speared some pasta on a fork, balanced a plate on her lap, and decided to try and make amends for her earlier faux pas.

"Mmmm…..this is a lovely sauce, Ria. Did you make it yourself?" She hoped against hope that her voice sounded genuinely thrilled.

"No, I just went over to Sainsbury's across the road and bought a jar. I hate cooking. I wish we could all just take a pill every day and be done with it." Ria picked up a slice of pizza with her fingers and took a large bite.

"Oh, well, it tastes nice anyway." Arla dabbed at her mouth with a serviette. "Do you have a knife please?"

"Pick the pizza up with your fingers, Mum. We don't stand on ceremony here." Stuart laughed and reached out for another slice.

Arla tried to appear unconcerned at the molten cheese that was running down the fingers of her left hand. She was aware that Shelley was trying hard not to smirk as she stuffed a piece of pizza into her mouth. Using what was left of her serviette, Arla put down her fork and wiped her fingers.

"Well, that was lovely, Ria! Thanks very much." She sipped some water and wondered whether her son would ever get to eat healthy vegetables again.

"That's okay." Ria stood up. "There's *Death by Chocolate* for pudding if you like. I couldn't resist it at the supermarket."

"I'm a bit full now; maybe later." Arla flashed a smile that did not quite reach to her eyes. "Save me a piece."

It was with some relief that she heard Ric making excuses to leave around four o'clock. After saying their goodbyes she flopped wearily into the car and let out a breath.

"I'm so sleepy after all that stodge!" She yawned loudly.

"I quite enjoyed it. We should have pizza sometimes too." Ric started the car's engine.

"For Sunday lunch? You must be joking!" Arla looked at him in amazement. "Poor Stuart won't be able to get out of the armchair after a few years of that."

"I'm sure that's not all they eat." Ric looked over his shoulder and pulled away from the kerb.

"I'm not so certain. Look at the size of her; she's never eaten a vegetable in her life. Our grandchild will resemble an inflated dumpling by its first birthday." She shook her head in disgust.

"Stuart seems happy enough." Ric turned on the wipers as a few spots of rain hit the windscreen.

"That's because of all the sex, I expect. He's used to proper food; not all that crap." Arla turned towards him. "What do you think of her?"

"She seems pleasant enough. I think that as long as our son's happy then we can't ask for more, can we?"

"He could have done better." Arla's voice was bitter. "*We* never brought him up to eat pizza with his fingers for Sunday lunch."

CHAPTER 16

"WELCOME, ARLA. IT'S been a few weeks now; how have you been getting on? Have you thought about what we were discussing last time?" Toni Beecher smiled and looked down at her notebook.

"I did start to think about it, but then everything went out the window. I found out I'm going to be a grandmother in October; I'm still getting my head around the fact." Arla exhaled slowly.

"Congratulations!" Toni glanced up. "That's good news!"

"Yes, I suppose it is, but then it makes you realise you'll now be the older generation. My youth's gone, and sometimes I feel sad that I haven't accomplished everything I wanted to in this life." Arla crossed her legs and fiddled with the hem of her jumper.

"And what did you want to accomplish?" Toni looked at Arla inquisitively.

"Oh….you know…… I wanted to be the perfect mother, have a wonderful marriage, and a dazzling career." Arla laughed ruefully. "Life doesn't always turn out how you expect though, does it?"

"It all comes back to what we were discussing last time; choices. Life is made up of choices, some of our own choosing and others that are made for us." Toni nodded to emphasise her statement.

"You're right there; I chose Ric, but I didn't choose to have a mother-in-law like Edna." Arla chuckled. "And it's safe to say I would never have chosen Ria, my new daughter-in-law, either." She rolled her eyes heavenwards.

"Why not?" Toni looked at her with interest.

"They don't seem suited to me." Arla shook her head.

"How do you know?"

Toni's direct questioning was unsettling. Arla tried to think of an answer:

"I'm just going on gut instinct I

suppose." "On first impressions?" "Yes."

Arla nodded.

"Have you found that has worked in the past?"

"Sometimes; especially where Edna was concerned, although I did wonder whether Val liked me to begin with until her mind was poisoned by her mother. I guess I'll never know." Arla shrugged.

"How have you and your husband been getting along?" Toni poured herself a glass of water.

"Oh….so so. The problem with Edna I suppose will never be solved, but I find it annoying that he's accepted Ria already, and as I said, I *know* that she's not going to be any good for our son at all." Arla sighed and twisted her wedding band around.

"So you're both having a further difference of opinion regarding your daughter-in-law?" Toni stopped writing and looked up.

"Well…. not to sound too snobby, but she's thick. She's got a menial job as a checkout girl in the supermarket, and now she's pregnant she's going to give that up soon and will be living off my son. There's not a brain cell in the girl's head. My son has worked hard to get where he is in the bank, and now he's got to keep her for the rest of her life." Arla tried to keep the bitterness from her voice.

Toni un-crossed and re-crossed her legs.

"I assume though that your son has chosen to do this and is happy?"

"Well, yes he would be at the moment. He hasn't had many girlfriends, and I suppose it's all sex and more sex for him at the moment. When the passion has worn off, I'm worried that he'll look at her and see what I see."

"But again, that comes down to choice. We have to accept and embrace others' choices. You could look at this situation in a different way." Toni smiled.

"What's that?" Arla sighed.

"For instance you could see this as a chance to welcome your new daughter-in-law into the family, and to make sure the relationship gets off to a better start than it did with yourself and your own mother-in-law. It looks as though your son has already chosen his life partner; do you think that in time you might be able to get to know her and accept his choice?

"It's easier said than done." Arla raised the palms of her hands. "We're worlds apart. We have nothing in common."

"Yes, you do." Toni smiled.

"What?" Arla replied with some irritation.

"You love your son as much as your daughter-in-law does. Your son thinks the world of you both, and I expect would love it if the two of you got along, especially now there's a new baby on the way."

"The trouble is, I have to take second place *again* in his life now; it's so hard getting used to it." Arla looked down at the carpet. "I was his whole world once, and now *she* is. I don't feel I'm the most important person in *anyone's* life now. I've been cast aside; made redundant."

"Do you think it's possible that maybe your mother-in-law could have had those exact same feelings when you married her son all those years ago?" Toni pressed on, peeped under her fringe, and tried to make eye contact.

The words struck Arla like a thunderbolt. She looked up into the counsellor's bright eyes:

"No doubt what you're saying *is* true. When I was young I never thought about the effect on Edna of Ric leaving home. We were too wrapped up in each other; I claimed Ric as mine to the world without even considering what his mother felt about it, and I suppose she must have been jealous and never forgave me for taking him away from her."

"There's certainly food for thought there." Toni nodded. "Can you see any similarities in your present day situation?"

Arla sighed and laced her fingers on her lap:

"Only last week Ric was going on about me not assuming it was Stuart ringing any more when I see his landline number on the caller display screen. I stopped phoning Edna a long time ago because she always said 'Hello Richard' when she picked up the phone. I've just done the self-same thing without thinking; I suppose it's because I always want it to be Stuart calling instead of Ria."

"That's understandable of course." Toni nodded again. "But now perhaps you'll be able to look at your relationship with Ria in a new light, taking into account all the issues you experienced at the start of your own marriage."

"Thanks. It's been a very helpful session today. Perhaps Edna should have had something like this twenty eight years ago." Arla smiled and fished in her bag for her purse.

"See if you can persuade your husband to come back next time." Toni jotted down some last-minute notes. "I prefer working with both partners."

"I'll try, but I don't think there's much more that can be done on that front." Arla shook her head.

"You'll be surprised just what can be achieved if both parties are willing and co-operative." Toni glanced up at Arla from her notebook.

"Stuart and I have had differences of opinion over the years, but as you know, all his life Ric has never said anything that would upset Edna. He's too old to change now." Arla shrugged.

"Again, you'd be surprised. If he's willing, we have all the time in the world to get to find out the reason behind why your husband will never argue with his mother."

"I don't think *he* knows; that's just the way he is. He's a closed book on that subject."

Toni took two twenty pound notes from Arla's outstretched hand:

"Well, we'll just have to try and open the book won't we? Goodbye for now, and thanks for the prompt payment."

"Goodbye, and thanks again." Arla's tone was lighter than usual.

"I really think I'm getting somewhere with Toni now." Arla lay facing Ric in bed. "Will you come back with me next time?"

"No; I'm done with all that."

"Will you not give it some thought?"

"Why? What's the use? We get nowhere."

"She's very astute, that Toni. She knows how to worm things out of you that you didn't even know yourself."

"For forty pounds a throw she'll keep worming until she can't worm any more." Ric yawned. "I'm knackered; night night."

"Night, night."

CHAPTER 17

"WELL?"

Stuart's upbeat voice at the other end of the phone line made her smile.

"Well what?"

"What do you think of Ria?"

"She seems like a nice girl." Arla hoped her voice sounded enthusiastic. "Where did you meet?"

"Every time I went into my local supermarket, she would be there on the checkout till. We started chatting, and well, one thing led to another."

It certainly did. Arla wished that her son could have perhaps visited an alternative establishment.

"I'm sure you've thought all this through? Marriage is a big step."

"Mum; she's having my baby!"

"I know, but I wanted to be sure that you're getting married because you want to and not just because of the baby."

"Don't you like her?" Stuart's voice had taken on a sulky tone.

"Of course I do, but I don't want you getting married in a hurry and regretting it for the rest of your life."

"I won't be; I love her, and she loves me."

Arla sighed silently and fiddled with the phone wire:

"Was the pregnancy planned?" She thought she already knew the answer to that question.

"No, but we're over the moon about it. Ria's going to make a wonderful mum. Don't worry; be happy for me."

"I am happy, Stuart. I just need to know that *you* are."

"I've never been happier. Look, I realise you don't know Ria that well, but give it time and you'll see why she's the only girl for me."

"Doesn't she want to go back to work after the baby's born?"

"No; she only ever wanted to be a mum. We don't want somebody else bringing up our child. Ria's the one to do it."

Her son's tone of voice was quite insistent. Arla knew when she was beaten:

"I hope you'll be very happy together. Let us know what we can pay for as regards the wedding."

"Oh, nothing. Ria's mum Mandy is quite well off; she phoned yesterday to let us know she's paying for everything." "Wow; that's a relief for you!" Arla felt a surge of jealousy shoot through her veins.

"We don't intend to sponge off Mandy though for the rest of our lives."

"No, of course not. I just meant it's a relief for you not to have to pay for the wedding with all the expense of a new baby as well." Arla hoped her explanation sounded plausible. "Can Dad and I pay for something for the baby instead, then?"

"I think Mandy's got that all sewn up as well, but I'll let you know on that one."

"How come Mandy's got so much money and Ria was just working as a checkout girl?" Arla could have bitten her tongue out as soon as she had spoken.

"What's wrong with working in a supermarket? It's what Ria wanted to do." Stuart's voice had risen slightly higher.

"Oh, God; I didn't mean it like that. I just think it's odd that somebody with a lot of money wouldn't have wanted to put her daughter through University."

"Ria's not University material."

"Oh." Not for the first time, Arla wondered what on earth her son saw in the girl.

"She's the one for me, Mum. In time you'll see why."

"I'm sure I will."

There was a slight pause before Stuart, bonhomie restored, asked his next question:

"What does Dad think of Ria?"

"Oh, you know your father; he doesn't have much of an opinion about anything."

"But he likes her?"

"Yes, as far as I know. He's very accepting as you're well aware, and is content to let people do just what they want to."

"Yeah; I got the feeling he likes her though."

"Yes, I'm sure he does, even though he never voices an opinion on any subject."

"Why?"

"Who knows? It's just the way he is."

"Okay then Mum; see you soon. Love you."

"Bye, love you too."

"Bye."

CHAPTER 18

THE PARK WAS bustling on a Spring Sunday afternoon in April. Arla sat on a bench next to Ric and watched as mothers restrained toddlers from picking the council daffodils.

"Next year that'll be us with our grandson or granddaughter, providing Ria lets us babysit. Do you think it'll be a boy or a girl?" Arla turned towards him.

"I don't know; perhaps it'll be one of each. I'm sure they'll only be too pleased for a night off once in a while; I know we were." Ric stretched his legs out in front of him. "Those first few years were a nightmare."

"It was good to be needed though." Arla sighed. "I think it's a boy."

"I still need you." Ric slipped his hand in hers and gave it a squeeze. "Don't forget that."

"Why? Why do you need me?" She looked at him.

"You're my wife; I love you." He shrugged. "Isn't that enough reason?"

"Yes, but you don't *need* me as such. If I walked out of this park and never went home again you'd still carry on living your life." She gave a return squeeze.

"Yeah; but I'd be one hell of a miserable bugger." He put his arm around her shoulders. "I need you in my life to make me happy."

She restrained herself from jumping up to comfort a small boy who had run on ahead of his parents and fallen over in front of her. As the child cried out and his mother rushed towards him, Arla's mind wandered back twenty years.

"Stuart was clumsy like that. He was always falling over." She reminisced. "Where's *my* little boy?"

"He's all grown up now and about to have a little one of his own."

"Sometimes I want him back, just to have a little warm hand to hold." She smiled inwardly at past memories.

"If it's any consolation you can hold mine." Ric chuckled. "Or there's something else that hasn't been held for a while either."

"Do you have to bring sex into every facet of the conversation?" She sighed. "Look; I know I haven't made you very happy lately."

"Likewise; although I think I must have ballsed it up from the start." Ric exhaled slowly.

"Toni talks much sense; I'm learning a lot from her." "Such as?" He turned towards her.

"Mainly that I have to accept things I can't change, instead of trying to control everything and everybody."

"You don't control me."

"I know; but many times I've tried to turn you around to my way of thinking. Toni tells me that people choose how they want to live, and I have to realise that I can't interfere with that."

"Just go with the flow, so to speak?"

"Yeah, I suppose so. She wants me to turn the tables around so that Ria and I can have a good relationship." She gave a wry laugh.

"Come on, let's take a walk." He stood up. "My arse is getting numb sitting here."

He bent down to pick up a stray daffodil lying morosely on its side on the grass.

"A token of my love. I know it looks a bit battered, but then so am I."

"Thanks." She laughed. "We're both a bit worn around the edges now."

She broke off part of the long stalk and secured the remainder of the daffodil to her buttonhole.

"Can we wander alongside the stream? I love that walk."

"Sure."

Holding hands they followed a gravel footpath as it led downwards past spindly lime trees on either side, not yet boasting their summer plumage. The sun's weak rays shone in her face, and Arla enjoyed the moment of togetherness.

"Would you reconsider coming back with me to see Toni? She's so wise, and I think it'll be good for us." She held her breath and nudged a stone with her foot in his direction.

"For Christ's sake, what for?" He kicked the stone back to her with increased force.

"Just to get some closure on all of this." She tapped the stone to him again.

"I'm willing to draw a line under it all now. I don't need to pay another forty pounds for the privilege." He sighed and launched the stone into the river.

"I'll use my savings; it's important to me. Please?" She squeezed his hand.

"Oh alright; fuck it." He looked up at the sky. "Don't use your savings; get it out of the joint account."

"Thanks; thanks so much." She smiled.

"My pleasure, I'm sure."

"Love you." She looked up at him.

"Love you too."

CHAPTER 19

THE FOUR BRUSSELS sprouts had cooled on his plate into hard, green balls of bitterness. He sat on his hands and traced the leafy pattern on the tablecloth with his eyes.

"Finish up your dinner, Richard; you're not leaving the table until you do."

"I don't like sprouts." He shook his head.

"Dad works hard to put food on the table; it's the least you can do to eat it." Edna glowered at her son from her chair on the opposite side of the dining table.

"I'll be sick." Seven year old Ric could already taste the bile in his throat.

"Eat your dinner!" Edna shouted and thumped the table with her fist.

"I'll eat them, Mum." Jan reached over with her fork.

"You will not! Your brother needs to learn obedience. If you and Valerie have finished, then off you go."

He saw the sympathetic smiles from his sisters as they left the table, all the while registering how the bullet-like brassicas seemed to look up at him with increased malevolence.

"I've got nothing to do this afternoon. We shall sit here until you've eaten them, or you'll be getting them back for your tea, that's for sure."

The ticking of a carriage clock on the mantelpiece was all that could be heard in the deathly silence of the room. His keen ears picked out Ronnie shouting to somebody outside whilst cycling up and down the road; the boy's carefree tones seemingly only adding to the hopelessness of his own miserable situation.

He stared at his plate and wished that he could magically transport the sprouts to another dimension, like they did in Star Trek when Captain Kirk shouted 'Beam me up, Scotty'. After hearing three dings of the carriage clock signalling that half the afternoon had already gone, he realised something had to be done in order to receive a piece of the jam sponge cake for tea that he had seen cooling on the window sill. He picked up his fork, swallowed hard, and with a shudder moved one hated sprout slowly towards his mouth.

He closed his eyes to shut out her gloat of triumph. As the sprout touched his lips the smell of it caused his stomach to revolt. To his horror, the pork chop and roast potatoes that had previously slid down with ease, now spontaneously upchucked and erupted with venom over his mother's best lace tablecloth.

"Get upstairs in the bathroom and clean yourself up, you little shit! If you think you're getting any tea later on, then you can think again!"

He felt a slap around his face as he ran, but dodged a second blow. Reaching the toilet just in time he retched again until his stomach was empty, and let the tears slide silently down his cheeks now that he was out of her sight. After laying on the bathroom floor for a while to recover, he washed his face, cleaned his teeth, and threw his sick-covered clothes in the washing basket. Padding barefoot in his pants to his bedroom, he climbed onto his bed and fell into a fitful sleep.

He was awakened some time later by hearing the creak of his bedroom door opening. He sat up and smiled at the sight of a plate in his sister's hands.

"Here; this is my bit of cake, but I sneaked it out and saved it for you. Just don't tell Mum, whatever you do."

"Thanks, Val." He reached out and wolfed down the moist cake ravenously, which tasted delicious.

"Next time she gives you sprouts, slide them on my plate before she sees anything, or if you can't do that, mash them up with your potato. That's what I do. Jan's lucky in that her seat is near the window; if it's open and Mum's not looking, then she throws hers out." Val turned towards the door again. "Mum's calmed down now; it's safe to come out."

He found some clean shorts and his favourite Star Trek t-shirt. Creeping downstairs he sat close to Val and Jan on the settee and tried to learn the rules of Monopoly. His mother watched Coronation Street on TV, occasionally giggling like a schoolgirl or grunting at the brazenness of Elsie Tanner. Whilst the soap opera ran he remained silent, but was relieved to find his mother was in a better mood. He played with the red plastic Monopoly houses, and let Val roll the dice and move his iron for him. When the programme finished his mother stood up.

"There's a piece of jam sponge left over for you, Richard. I'll go and get it for you."

She made her way to the kitchen, and Ric grinned at his sisters. When he had eaten the second slice of cake his hunger pangs had subsided, and all that was left to do was to find out if he was still loved as much as his sisters.

"Can I have a cuddle please Mum?"

"Come on then."

Ignoring his sisters' smirks, he jumped up into his mother's lap before she could change her mind.

"Sorry I was sick; I couldn't help it." He closed his eyes and breathed in the warm scent of her, content with feeling her arms around him.

"Just don't do it again."

"I won't if you don't give me any more sprouts." He held his breath and waited for her reply that she would never ever give him another disgusting vegetable as long as she lived.

"You can just have the odd one or two. I'll put a bit of cheese sauce on them for you next time."

On hearing Jan's almost silent snort of laughter, he made a mental note to give his sister a kick.

CHAPTER 20

HIS NINE YEAR old legs could run like the wind. If he got a good speed up he could vault over the garden fence lickety-spit. After Jan had found the bullfrog in her bed, his mother's unrestrained rage at both himself and at her own inability to grab even the back of his collar caused him to bolt like greased lightning out of the front door and over the fence. He was off down the road in a matter of seconds, while his heart hammered a terrifying rhythm in his chest listening to her vituperative, vociferous threats as she lumbered along behind him.

With some relief he was aware that her voice had petered out as came nearer to the woods. Shinning up a tree with the practised ease of an athletic squirrel in the prime of its life, he squatted on a branch undercover of thick summer foliage, and waited.

After some time had passed and his legs were starting to cramp, he peeped out through the leaves; Ronnie Braithwaite was just about to cycle underneath his tree. Breaking off a twig he threw it down on his friend's head as Ronnie manoeuvred the stunt bike over a large tree root.

"Wanker!" Ric giggled and threw another twig.

"Oy!" Ronnie raised his head in the direction of the voice and grinned. "What you doing up there?"

"Have you seen my mum?" Ric glanced over Ronnie's head at the entrance to the woods.

"I knocked for you and she said you were

out." "So she's at home, yeah?" "Yeah."

Ronnie nodded.

Sighing with relief, Ric swung down expertly from the branch and landed on the leafy ground with a thud.

"She's mad at me. I put a frog in Jan's bed."

"Cool! Did she scream?" Ronnie looked at Ric in wonder.

"Loud enough to bring Mum running upstairs. I had to leg it out here." Ric chuckled. "It was worth it though to see Jan's face. I thought her eyes were going to pop right out of her head."

"I wish I'd been there." Ronnie grinned again.

"I'm getting hungry now; I'm going back for some tea. I'll knock for you afterwards."

"Yeah; see you later then."

With some trepidation he sneaked in through the open back door. His mother stood at the kitchen table, sleeves rolled up and hands covered in flour.

"What are you making, Mum?" He nuzzled his nose into the top part of her fleshy arm, and then rested his cheek on her sleeve. "Can I have some?"

"It's a vegetable pie. I'm going to put lots of sprouts in it for you."

"Mmm…..nice!" His heart sank and he gave her a kiss.

"Don't try and get round me, you bloody nuisance. Go and say you're sorry to your sister."

"Okay."

Light-hearted with relief that he had escaped a worse fate, he went upstairs and found his sister sitting at her dressing table brushing her hair.

"Go away, you pig." Jan threw her brush in his direction.

"Sorry about the frog." He quickly sidestepped the missile.

"You're going to eat all my sprouts this evening. Mum's making a vegetable pie."

"Yeah; great. Bring it on." He picked up the brush and handed it to his sister.

"Don't you ever do that again." Jan gave him an icy stare enough to freeze the sea.

"I won't."

"Have you got round her yet? You always seem to manage it, whatever you do."

"All you have to do is give her a kiss and a cuddle." Ric shrugged.

"Toe-rag."

"Frog-hater."

Duty done, he went back down to ensure the dining room window was open as wide as it could go. His aim was now quick and true; his mother was always bustling in and out of the kitchen during dinner; by the morning something or someone would have always managed to clear up all the foul-smelling, bitter evidence.

CHAPTER 21

"SO YOU QUICKLY grew wise to the fact that instead of sitting for hours at the table, you could throw any food out of the window that you didn't want to eat without your mother knowing?" Toni Beecher chuckled.

"Absolutely. I used to chuck lorry loads of sprouts past Jan's head and out the window. It was sprout heaven in our garden at night for any creature who wanted them." Ric grinned, yawned, and stretched out his legs.

"Would you say that your mother's bark was worse than her bite?" Toni looked questioningly at Ric.

"Probably, although it took me a long time to find that out. If she caught you straight away you'd get a wallop, but I usually managed to duck her aim and run. By the time I came home for tea she'd usually calmed down."

"Were you frightened of her?"

Arla was aware of Ric shifting uncomfortably in his seat at Toni's direct questioning. He cleared his throat before replying.

"As a young kid, yes; but then as I grew older I realised I only had to butter her up and she was putty in my hands, so to speak. My sisters used to give her all the lip, and as I said previously they had some right old ding-dongs, but as far as I was concerned all I had to do was give her a cuddle. Dad was hardly ever there, and I suppose she liked the contact."

"We all could do with a cuddle now and then, that's for sure." Toni nodded. "Were you aware that she may have favoured you over your sisters?"

"Not to start with, but we did grow quite close, especially after Dad died and I was the only one left living at home."

"Do you think your sisters resented the preferable way you were treated?" Toni turned over a page of her notebook.

"Don't know really; after the usual teenage tantrums died down they both got on well with Mum, and she helped them out a lot after they were married and the babies started to come along."

Arla took hold of Ric's hand.

"I think we all know she favoured you the most. Tell Toni about the haystack incident."

"Oh, that's all water under the bridge now; I don't want to rake that up again." Ric sighed and shook his head.

"If it would help, perhaps it might be an idea?" Toni shrugged.

"It's just that I got in with a bad crowd when I was about fifteen. I suppose it was a forerunner of the gang culture that's prevalent today. I was young and silly, and looked up to the leader, a boy called Billy Newnham. Newcomers to the gang always had to go through some sort of initiation ceremony……..." He broke off and looked down at his hands.

"I see." Toni nodded. "Do you feel like sharing what you had to do to join the gang?"

"Oh, this is all old news now. I'm not proud of it in the least, but I set light to a haystack in the field across from our local woods. Billy was watching, so I had to do it. Somebody recognised us, and decided to call the fire brigade and the police." Ric sighed.

"What happened next?" Toni glanced over at Ric with interest.

"We legged it as soon as we heard the sirens coming up the road. I ran straight home. Mum was watching the TV, so I said a quick hello and went up to my room. I stank of smoke, so I had a quick shower and changed my clothes. It wasn't long before a copper came knocking on the door though." He gave a rueful smile at the memory.

"What did you do?" Toni took a sip of water.

"Nearly crapped myself, but put on a brave front as usual. Mum came up trumps and said I'd been at home all night with her. It was entirely due to her statement that I didn't end up with a caution and a police record."

"Did she suspect you'd had anything to do with it?" Toni jotted down notes and then looked up.

"Of course she knew; she wasn't silly. I realised with hindsight that my smoky clothes would have been a dead giveaway, but she never said anything more about it, other than she didn't want me going around with Billy Newnham anymore."

"And did you?" Toni smiled.

"No; I decided I owed her something for keeping quiet; plus the fact I now actually wanted to distance myself from Billy. I wonder where he is now? Banged up I expect." Ric chuckled.

Arla had heard the story many times, but this latest version she had witnessed from Ric's own lips seemed to fill the air with something other than regret.

"You've never mentioned to me before why you stopped seeing Billy." Arla gave his hand a squeeze.

"You don't like talking about my mum. I did it for her; I felt a complete prat afterwards and wanted to make amends. She had been rooting for me, and had stuck her neck out and lied to the police. I knew that whatever happened in the future she would be on my side, but I felt I'd let her down." He reached forward for a tissue. "It seems I was a shit of a son, and ended up being an even bigger shit of a husband."

To Arla's surprise she was aware that Ric's eyes had filled with tears.

"Are you okay Mr Deane? Do you want to carry on?" Toni put down her pen and notebook and looked at Ric with some concern.

"I think I've had enough for today. I don't know that this opening up of old wounds is doing any good." He sniffed and wiped his eyes.

"Oh, you'll be surprised in the long run." Toni smiled. "I can usually help most couples who come to see me."

"I'll take your word for it then."

Arla looked at Ric and took his hand.

"You've done really well today; let's go home

now." "I was hoping you'd say that."

On the way home Arla noticed that Ric meandered the car through the streets and just for once was not breaking all the speed limits.

"Did you get anything out of the counselling session today?" She felt safe enough to talk to him whilst he was driving.

"Don't know." Ric put the car in gear and pulled away from the traffic lights.

"I'll take that as a *yes* then." She smiled at him.

"Take it any way you want."

CHAPTER 22

"I'M SORRY YOU got upset this evening." She snuggled up against him in bed and put her arm across his chest.

"It's dredging all these ghosts up from the past; I'd rather stay in the present. Can we knock it on the head for tonight and just have a cuddle instead?" He put his arms around her and gave her a squeeze. "I love you; I'd go to the ends of the earth for you. If that's not enough, then I don't know what else I can do."

She loved the familiar hirsuteness of him. She stroked his chest hair, which proliferated in curly tufts all over the top half of his body:

"It's a shame I'm not a cat, 'cos if I was I'd be purring." He chuckled and lay still, enjoying the sensation.

"All I'm going to say about it is that earlier on with Toni I thought we might be getting somewhere. I can't wait to go back tomorrow. Can I carry on stroking your chest?" She looked up at him.

"Be my guest." He sighed and closed his eyes.

After a while, the warmth of his body against her cheek was soporific. Arla slid her arm around his waist and moved one leg to rest over the top of his thighs:

"We haven't laid like this for a long time. I'd forgotten how nice it is." She exhaled slowly, savouring his smell of soap and talcum powder.

"I know something else that's nice as well." He turned towards her. "How about I do the same for you?"

"Do what?"

"Stroke your chest."

"If you like." She giggled. "Turn over on your back then."

His hands were warm and surprisingly soft. Arla sank back into the pillows and remembered times when they could not get enough of each other; his body draining her energy with its demands. She tried but failed to remember the last time they had made love, but tonight she was aware that after comforting him following his latest revelations, she was feeling strangely aroused.

She sighed and closed her eyes, enjoying the feel of his hands gently skimming over her breasts. Raising her back so that the nipples were more prominent, a small moan of pleasure escaped from her lips, which she was relieved to find did not go undetected. She felt her husband's lips encircle one nipple and then its jealous companion; his gentle licking and sucking causing her to arch her back even further to create a delicious tension that she had almost forgotten existed. When his tongue traced a slow line downwards towards her pubic hair she parted her knees so that he could see her engorged clitoris, throbbing almost painfully and eager for release:

"Kneel in front of me; I remember how you like it."

His hot whispering in her ear excited her even more. She turned over and knelt, holding onto the bedhead with her left hand. She felt his arm slide around her waist, helping her to remain steady. His penis dug urgently into the small of her back, and moving her right hand backwards she felt its hardened muscular contractions as she moved her hips wider and guided it inside her.

"Jeez! That feels so good, darling!"

She smiled and gripped the back of his neck with her right hand and tipped her head back, exalting in the closeness of him. When his finger rubbed her clitoris she spread her hips as wide as they would go, moving with him in perfect unison to create a shuddering release that for the first time in almost thirty years perfectly coincided with his own.

"I love you so much, Arla. That was amazing! I'd do anything for you."

He slumped forward onto her back. She moved onto all fours and then sank back down, sated and enjoying the brief weight of his entire body.

"I love you too, but if you don't get off me I'm going to suffocate….."

He laughed and flopped onto the pillow, glad to be rid of the tension between them. She snuggled into his arms and slept the best dreamless sleep that she had had in a long time.

CHAPTER 23

"IT'S BEEN OVER a week now; how have the two of you been getting on?" Toni Beecher smiled at them and took a pen from her clipboard.

"Not too bad actually." Arla tried to keep as straight a face as possible. "Quite well in fact."

"That's good to hear. Last time we had some insight into Ric's relationship with his mother, and how that has affected his choices and decisions in life. We'll focus on you more this time, Arla. How did you feel following Ric's revelations?"

The clock began ticking the minutes of the session away. Arla looked towards Ric and slid her hand in his.

"I never realised he's felt guilty all these years that his mother had lied to the police for him."

"So it was a shock in fact, to find out how he felt." Toni nodded and opened her notebook.

"Yes, but then again, isn't that what mothers are supposed to do? Stick up for their children against all odds?" Arla shrugged.

"Would you have done the same for your own son?" Toni looked up at Arla.

"Lied to the police?"

"Yes." Toni nodded.

"Well, it would have depended on what he'd done, I suppose." Arla looked at Ric, who remained non-communicative.

"Hypothetically then; what if your son had murdered somebody, and you found out about it?" Toni crossed her legs and swung one foot back and forth.

"That's a toughie……." Arla appeared temporarily flummoxed.

"Your statement to the police could cause him to be jailed for the rest of his natural life." Toni looked from one to the other.

"If push comes to shove…….no, I wouldn't inform the police. What about you, Ric?" Arla looked over for support.

"I think it depends on the circumstances. If he was a serial killer, then yes, I think I would. If he'd murdered in self-defence, then no." Ric shrugged.

"Exactly; we need to find reasons for certain behaviours to obtain closure. Arla, do you feel you have found the reason behind Ric's treatment of his mother?" Toni looked up from her notebook.

"I think so; there's probably more than one reason though, and also possibly others that I'm not aware of. Maybe he's always felt indebted to her for saving him from having a police record, but then also feels guilty for letting her down and bringing shame on the family."

"Ric; do you think Arla's assumptions may be correct?" Toni turned towards Ric.

"Don't know; I've not really given it much thought." Ric clammed up and folded his arms across his chest.

"I wonder sometimes if it's *me* who's been the problem all along." Arla sighed.

"Why do you say that?" Toni looked at Arla with interest.

"Ric's so *accepting* of everything and everybody. Perhaps it's me; maybe I'm the jealous type? He's pointed out recently where I've done exactly the same thing as my mother-in-law." Arla nodded in confirmation.

"What was that?" Toni took a sip of water.

"I didn't realise I was answering the phone just like *she* does. It hit home to me that I didn't know I was saying '*Hello Stuart'* when I picked up the receiver and not waiting to see if it was Ria or not. I'd become so used to it only being Stuart living there, you see." Arla exhaled. "I was horrified."

"But there's one good thing to consider." Toni leaned forward and smiled.

"What?"

"You're now aware you're doing this. Tell me; how's your self-confidence? Do you suffer with low self-esteem?"

Arla sipped some water and wrestled with her emotions.

"It's true I don't have a lot of self-confidence. I often wonder whether the problems we have could have been my fault all along. Is it natural to never say anything controversial towards one's mother? It's unnatural for me, I can assure you."

"It's not all your fault; it's mine too. I've already said I've been a shit husband." Ric stood up. "Can we leave it for today? This isn't getting us anywhere and I don't want it to deteriorate into another argument when we get home."

"It won't; I promise. If you really want to leave then we'll go, but I have the feeling we're just starting to get somewhere." Arla gave Ric's hand a squeeze.

"Come back and see me in a few days when you've had another chance to talk." Toni stood up. "You can have this one at half the price."

"Thanks." Arla fished in her purse. "See you later in the week then."

On returning home she could see there was a missed call on the landline display screen, but no message. As she peered down to recognise the number, the phone rang again. She bit her lip, put the receiver to her ear, and stopped herself just in time.

"Hello?"

"Hi Arla, it's Ria. Was your mobile switched off?"

"Oh, hello there! How's it going?" She by-passed the question and hoped she sounded cheerful enough.

"Great, thanks. I'm going shopping for baby things on Saturday, and I wondered if you wanted to come along?"

"Me?"

"Of course! The baby will be your grandchild! I thought you might like to help me choose the pram? My mum's coming as well; she'll be paying for everything, so don't worry on that aspect."

Ria's excited voice sounded as though she was about twelve years old. Arla smiled at the young woman's excitement, and felt genuinely pleased.

"Yes…thanks… I'd love to! Where shall I meet you?"

"I've decided a good place to go is the Whitgift Centre in Croydon. There's loads of shops there. Is it too far for you? Come for lunch first if you like, and then we can all go in the same car afterwards."

"Okay; thanks for asking me. I'm looking forward to it."

"Same here!"

She put the phone down and smiled:

"Who was that?" Ric hung the car keys up on a hook.

"Ria. She wants me to go shopping with her on Saturday for the baby's pram."

"Great stuff."

As she got ready for bed that evening, she brought her mind around again to the therapy sessions, and how the chasm between them seemed to be eroding by the day.

"Any time you feel like stroking my titties again, feel free." Ric chuckled and slipped an arm around Arla's shoulders under the bedcovers.

"Look where it got us last time." She buried her face in his chest hair.

"Exactly!" He squeezed her shoulder. "Can we give counselling a miss now? We don't really need it anymore, do we?"

Arla looked up at him.

"I'd like to go just once or twice more if that's okay with you? I've realised after all this time that it's not just the issues with you and your mum; I'm also contributing to the problem. I think I've obviously got a jealous nature; Mum told me years ago during a big bust-up that jealousy would be my downfall, and I remember shouting at her to shut up and stop talking rubbish." She sighed and cuddled up to him. "It's probably been me all along and not you."

"That's where you're wrong." He sat up in bed and clasped his arms around his knees.

"I've been trying to control you all these years, but you've never done that to me. I've got to listen to Toni and become more accepting of everyone, like you." She sat up next to him; touching his bare arm with her own.

"Look; if I wanted to do something, nothing and nobody in this world is going to stop me." He rested his chin on his knees. "You're not controlling me; it's all a load of bollocks."

"I know that if you wanted to run off with Mrs Nugent next door I couldn't stop you, but I've been trying to make you choose me over your mum by using a sort of emotional blackmail. That's just as bad; I'm so sorry." She leaned towards him and sighed.

"Ann Nugent? Good God, I'd have to be desperate!" He sat up straighter and chuckled. "Have you seen her lately?"

"Figuratively speaking." Arla grinned.

"Stop beating yourself up about us; you've been an excellent wife to me all these years. I told you; it's me." He lay back down on the pillows.

"Why? Why do you say that?" She propped herself up on one elbow and looked down at him.

"Something happened a long time ago, but I don't want to talk about it."

"I'm sure you'll feel a lot better if you got it off your chest." She lay down with him and slid an arm around his waist.

"Forget it; we've all got our cross to bear. Just take it from me that I'm as guilty as you, and then we can move forward and live happily ever after." He pulled her to him. "Just remember I love you; I've always loved you, and by the way I'm not going to run off with Ann Nugent."

"I'm very pleased to hear it."

She lifted her face to his and enjoyed a long, lingering kiss. When at length he rolled on top of her she wrapped her legs around his back and welcomed the closeness and the feel of his penis inside her. His recent revelation had started a myriad of questions burning in her brain, and her mind was elsewhere. She looked at her husband's face; eyes were closed and head was tipped back in ecstasy. However, even with his whispered endearments and urgent thrusting against her, she felt about as aroused as a sack of potatoes. After feeling his release, she stroked his hair as he sank back down on top of her.

"Did you come?" He sucked gently on her nipple. "Yes."

She whispered and hoped it sounded convincing enough.

"I love you; I'll always love you." He kissed her forehead and rolled off her onto the bed.

"Love you too darling."

CHAPTER 24

"NO RIC THIS evening?" Toni looked questioningly at Arla standing on the doorstep. "Come in out of the cold."

"Ric's had to work late, but I still wanted to see you." Arla took off her coat and followed Toni into the consulting room.

"Take a seat, Arla. I thought then that this time we'd talk about *your* childhood if that's okay with you?" Toni made herself comfortable and opened her notebook.

"There's not much to tell really." Arla shrugged and sat down.

"Have you got any brothers or sisters?" Toni smiled at her.

"No; Mum always said I was an evil child and I put her off having any more kids."

"Isn't that a bit harsh?" Toni chuckled.

"I was a bit strong-willed; I had my own ideas and opinions, and she had hers. We argued terribly, but I grew up and we get along fine now."

"How about your dad? Was he strict?" Toni chewed the end of her pen.

"He was a pussycat really; he tended to leave me to Mum to handle. He'd only come in with the rough stuff if I was really out of line."

"Rough stuff?"

"Well, he smacked me a few times, but I daresay I deserved it." Arla nodded.

"Did you have lots of friends as a child?" Toni poured some water from a jug into two glasses.

"No, not too many; enough so that there was always somebody to play with though."

"Were you okay with sharing your toys?"

"Not really; what was mine was mine, so to speak." Arla chuckled. "I suppose that's the problem a lot of only children have; they're no good at sharing."

"Yes, I have come across this situation a few times before." Toni nodded. "Tell me, did you feel threatened by Ric's family when you were first introduced to them?"

"Threatened?" Arla looked blank.

"Let me put it another way; were you jealous at all of the relationship Ric already had with his mother and sisters?

Arla felt uneasy that Toni was hedging too close to the truth. She panicked slightly on realising the counsellor might think something along the lines of her being a twisted, envious bitch. She wondered suddenly if the entire twenty eight year scenario had been fuelled by her excessively jealous nature.

"No, not at all. Dad told me I was marrying Ric and not his family. I tended to keep Edna and his sisters in the background really." She exhaled silently and hoped that she had got away with it.

"Did you wish for brothers and sisters as a child?" Toni delved a bit deeper.

"No, not really; I was happy being the centre of Mum and Dad's world." Arla smiled.

"Do you think you might have looked for the same adulation in your adult relationships?" Toni made sure to hit the nail right on the head.

"Adulation?" Arla played for time.

"Wanting to be the centre of your husband and children's worlds."

"I suppose it makes sense; I never really thought about it like that." Arla felt embarrassed and ashamed. "Oh God, is everything my fault?" She put her hand to her mouth.

"As with most couples it's usually six of one and half a dozen of the other." Toni smiled. "The trick is to learn your failings and try to put things right."

"Well, I'm meeting up with my daughter-in-law-to-be at the weekend." Arla nodded. "It looks like I need to have a go at trying to change my outlook."

"Super!" Toni clapped her hands together. "Let me know how you get on."

Arla could hardly concentrate on the remainder of the session. All she could think about was the jealous nature that Toni had so cleverly winkled out of her. How could she, Arla, not have realised that all the problems they had ever gone through over the years regarding Ric's family had been her fault all along?

CHAPTER 25

"ARLA, MEET MY mum Mandy; Mum, this is Arla, Stu's mum."

Arla came face-to-face with an older, overly made up, impeccably groomed and heavily perfumed lookalike of her new daughter in law.

"Hi Mandy!"

Arla hoped she looked younger as she stepped forward into the hallway to give the rather stout-looking woman a hug. She could see Mandy's grey roots peeking through the light brown dye, and gave silent thanks for her own recent visit to the hairdresser.

"Pleased to meet you! I must say straight away what a lovely son you have!" Mandy gushed as she returned the hug.

"We think so!" Arla grinned. "It seems that before too long we're going to be related."

"I'm so excited! Ria phones me every night with the latest news; I can't wait to be a grandmother!"

"Is Stuart at home today, Ria?" Arla looked past the two women into an empty kitchen.

"He's out setting up his drums; the band have got a gig tonight down at the pub on the high street."

"Ah, I see. It's a shame then; I'm going to miss him."

"You can always come to the gig if you like?" Ria looked at Arla expectantly.

"No, no! I'm a bit old for all that. He'd be appalled to see his mother there." Arla laughed. "I'm looking forward to the shopping trip though."

"Come in and have some sandwiches and cake first. I'll put the kettle on. Go in and talk to Mum and I'll bring the lunch through."

Arla tried to ignore the small stab of jealousy she felt at the thought of the mother and daughter talking nightly on the telephone. She felt guilty as she tried to remember the last time she had called her own mother, or picked up the phone to hear the welcome sound of Shelley's voice. Suddenly she realised that in the last few months she had taken more calls from Ria than she had from her own mother or daughter.

"Your daughter seems like a very outgoing, loving person." Arla stated with genuine warmth.

"Oh, everybody loves Ria. She sees the best in people." Mandy nodded and smiled.

"Our family tends to be a little bit anti-social. Ria's going to be a breath of fresh air." Arla stopped short of stating her own inadequacies.

"She's got at least five thousand friends on Facebook; every time she posts something she gets hundreds of likes straight away." Mandy laughed, settled into an armchair, and crossed her legs.

"I'm not on Facebook, but I can see that somebody with Ria's personality is going to attract others to her."

"She's like her father, God rest his soul. I fell in love as soon as I saw him." Mandy appeared wistful. "He died last year and I miss him every single day."

"Oh, I'm sorry." Arla perched herself on the edge of the settee.

"Ria's been a huge support to me. I don't know what I'd have done without her. She and immersing myself in work got me through a rather tough time." Mandy nodded.

"Where do you work?" Arla looked at Mandy with interest.

"I'm a psychiatrist. I have a clinic at my local hospital in Croydon, near where we're going today actually."

"Really? That must be fascinating! How did you find juggling work with looking after Ria?" Arla hid her surprise as best she could.

"People often ask me that." Mandy chuckled. "I had the most wonderful husband who stayed at home to look after her. I only wanted to go through pregnancy once, and was never really very maternal, so Donald let me work. I earned more money than him anyway, so it made sense for him to be the house-husband. What do you do?"

Arla felt inadequate under the stare of such a formidable woman:

"I – I gave up nursing many years ago to bring up Stuart and his sister Shelley. I've always done Ric's invoicing though; he's a self-employed plumber."

"Good for you; I admire anyone who can give up a career for their children. I suppose I was too selfish to do that, but Ria hasn't turned out too badly. She has her father's temperament, and the most beautiful thing about her is that she is happy with her lot, as was Donald. It's a joy to see my daughter in love and planning for motherhood." Mandy smiled.

"Did you dream that maybe she might want to follow you into the medical profession some day?" Arla looked for disappointment on Mandy's face.

"Absolutely not. Ria is her daddy's girl over and over. I'm just happy that she's doing what she always wanted to do." Mandy nodded to emphasise her point.

"Are you two getting to know each other?" Ria came in and set down a plate of sandwiches on the table. "Arla, you'll find Mum and I are not similar at all, yet we get on like a house on fire."

"You're very similar to look at." Arla smiled.

"Yes, but that's where it ends. Mum's a high flyer; I only ever wanted marriage and motherhood." Ria handed out cups of tea.

"You'll be an excellent mother, I'm sure." Arla nodded and took a few sips of tea.

"I sometimes wish I'd had more children now, for Ria's sake." Mandy took a plate and a sandwich. "But at the time I couldn't face another pregnancy and all the time off work."

"You could have paid me to look after all my brothers and sisters." Ria laughed. "There's still time, Mum. You're not menopausal yet."

"Oh goodness me, no; what a thought – a mother again at forty five!" Mandy's high-pitched laugh echoed around the room. "I'd need a man to start with!"

"That can be arranged." Ria helped herself to a sandwich. "Try Internet dating; it works. It's how I met Stu."

Arla nearly fell off the settee in surprise.

"You met through a dating agency?"

"Sure; everyone does it these days." Ria shrugged. "Didn't Stu tell you?"

"He'd probably go to great lengths *not* to tell me." Arla chuckled. "I was under the impression you met him when he came into the supermarket where you work."

"No; I don't work near enough to where he lives. I think we were both searching for each other. The computer matched us up; I got Stu, and he got me!" Ria's laugh tinkled like a piano. "We've got the same sort of personality; both of us are quite laid-back, and neither of us are keen on confrontations. I found out that Stu was looking for a homely girl."

"He couldn't have found a more home-loving girl than you, that's for sure." Mandy laughed and chomped on a sandwich.

Arla was taken aback. All the dreams she had of her son meeting some high-flying bank executive and producing a string of brilliant and talented children took a nosedive with the realisation that, true to form, he had purposely searched for a girl who was the exact opposite to the dream she had envisaged. She nibbled on a ham and tomato sandwich and sighed.

CHAPTER 26

"THIS IS BIGGER than Westen's shopping centre. Is it always this busy?" Arla looked about her at the hundreds of shoppers dashing to and fro, laden with purchases.

"Most of the time, yeah." Ria nodded. "Is shopping not your thing?"

"Oh, I don't mind; I'm game, as long as my knees hold out." Arla laughed.

"And my back." Mandy winced. "We'll have to have a coffee break soon."

"We've only just got here!" Ria rolled her eyes. "Come on; I want to have a look in Mothercare."

Inside the store Arla concealed a hot stab of envy at the sight of dreamy, self-satisfied-looking ladies, some clearly at a very advanced stage of pregnancy. She remembered her own two babies, the lack of spare cash, and second hand prams and baby clothes from boot sales. Her new grandchild would want for nothing.

"We have to grab Mum while she's not busy." Ria chuckled and winked at Mandy. "She'll soon get fed up with this."

"I'm only too pleased it's not me going through it all again." Mandy laughed. "Once was enough."

"I regret not having more kids now." Arla replied. "But at the time two was enough to cope with; not to mention the expense of it all."

"We want three ideally." Ria nodded. "Four if possible."

"Bloody hell; you're brave! Wait until you've had two and then have a re-think!" Arla recalled Shelley and Stuart's constant bickering and fighting. "You end up being a dawn 'til dusk referee."

"My kids won't fight." Ria replied confidently.

"That's what I said to start with." Arla gave a mock shudder. "Sometimes I wanted to buy the pair of them boxing gloves and tell them to go outside and sock each other one."

"Why didn't you?" Ria looked at Arla with interest.

"Because although Stuart was younger, he was definitely stronger, and we were trying to teach him to treat girls with respect."

"Well, he does, so you obviously managed it."

"Yeah, but it took years. Kids are like little savages; they've got to be tamed."

Mandy, her attention span waning, viewed the array of pushchairs with only half an interest.

"So, what one do you want then?"

"Mum, I don't even know yet; I'm still looking. Which one do you like, Arla?"

"That one over there." Arla pointed to an expensive-looking contraption which seemed to have more than one function. "It can turn into a baby seat or a carry-cot as well."

"Does it do the night feeds too?" Mandy yawned and checked her iPhone. "Or change slimy nappies?"

"Yeah, it does; and it finds that long-lost bung in the early hours of the morning that fell out of the baby's mouth and woke it up." Arla guffawed.

"Will you two pack it in?" Ria admonished. "You're no help at all."

"Sorry, daughter; I'm all ears." Mandy put her phone away. "We're just trying to discolour those rose-tinted spectacles you're wearing."

"Yeah; sort of break you in gently." Arla nodded.

"You don't frighten me; I'm going to play it by ear and see what happens. I think I'll go for that pram over there actually." Ria pointed to a pushchair that had not been previously favoured by either her mother or Arla. "It's not as expensive as the others, yet it's got everything I'm looking for."

"Then let's go for it." Mandy yawned again. "I'm dying for a cup of tea."

Arla heard Mandy sigh as she settled down at Costa Coffee with a steaming brew, and not for the first time wondered at the impracticality of the woman's designer stilettos.

"Better?"

"Yes thanks, Arla. My feet are killing me."

"You need some trainers for this job." Arla chuckled. "Like mine." She lifted one foot from under the table.

"I can't wear flatties; I've always worn high heels for work."

"I'm the opposite; my ankles twist over if I wear heels and I go base over apex."

"Mum always looks like she's going out for the evening, even if she's just got out of bed." Ria laughed.

“What would my patients say if I turned up wearing a tracksuit and trainers?” Mandy roared. “I’ve got to make an impression.”

“Not with me; you’re my mum. For our next shopping trip I want to see you in jogging bottoms and a pair of designer trainers.”

“With the size of my behind, I think it’s probably best that we skip the joggers.” Mandy warmed her hands around her cup. “However, you never know; I’ll see if I can buy a pair of flatter stilettos.”

“Isn’t that what they call an oxymoron?” Arla laughed. “I

wouldn’t know.” Ria shrugged. “I was never any good at English at school.”

CHAPTER 27

"HAVE YOU HAD a good week?" Toni poured some water into three glasses.

"Different; I went out shopping with my daughter-in-law-to-be and her mother last Saturday." Arla took off her coat and put it over the arm of the two-seater settee.

"How was it different?" Toni smiled.

"Well, I found out something about our son that knocked me for six." Arla crossed her legs and slipped Ric's hand in hers.

"Would you like to share it?" Toni looked up expectantly from her notebook.

Arla glanced at Ric, who shrugged.

"He met Ria through an Internet dating site. It turns out he was looking for an earth-mother homely type. She's definitely that." Arla nodded.

"Many people have met their partners in this way." Toni agreed. "How did you feel when you found out?"

"Shocked really, especially as he told me they'd met when he used to go into the supermarket where she worked. I thought only desperate people who couldn't find anybody joined Internet dating sites? Ric doesn't seem bothered by it, but I suppose I was hoping he was going to meet somebody at work who was more on his level."

"His intellectual level?" Toni enquired.

"Yes. I don't think Ria has any qualifications, you see. She's only been working at the checkout tills. I was disappointed."

Ric cleared his throat.

"She's what he wants. I've told you; it's serving no use to keep going on about it."

"It all comes down to accepting others' choices again, I know that." Arla sighed. "But I still can't help feeling sad that we struggled to bring Stuart up the best way we could and give him everything we never had, and he turns around and takes up with somebody who can't possibly be any asset to him in the future."

"Ooh, I don't know….. he's probably happy that his fiancée just wants to be a mother and will pose no challenge to him or his career in the long run." Ric nodded. "Stuart can rise through the ranks and he won't need to take a year's paternity leave just because Ria needs to go back to work."

"I never thought of it like that." Arla looked at him. "You ought to voice an opinion more often."

"Do you like your daughter-in-law?" Toni looked directly at Arla.

"I do actually, after having initial doubts when I first saw her. She's somebody who people warm to, and she has a very loving nature, I can see that. However, how is she going to aide my son in the business world and in the boardroom if he ever gets there?"

"The qualities you see in Ria are obviously what attracted your son to her in the first place. We all have a talent for something, and your daughter-in-law seems to possess people skills in abundance." Toni smiled.

"It's strange." Arla nodded. "Her mother is the complete opposite. She's a psychiatrist; not maternal at all, and dedicated to her work. She gave Ria money to buy a pram. I was there, and Ria asked both of us which pram we preferred. Her mother tried to look interested and pointed to the nearest one, and I gave my opinion, but Ria ultimately chose a different one completely. I asked myself why she wanted us there at all actually."

"Obviously for the company, I'd say." Ric shrugged. "If she's a people person then she probably wanted somebody around to bounce ideas off of or just to chat."

"I suppose so; she's just so different from me. I would have gone shopping on my own." Arla stared directly at Toni. "What's wrong with me? Why am I like this? Why am I such a jealous bitch?" She heaved another sigh and wiped a stray tear away. "Why am I so dissatisfied with everybody?"

She was aware that Ric had moved closer and had put his arm around her.

"You're not a bitch; stop beating yourself up. It's like Toni says; accept. It's all we can do. Stuart's happy with Ria, and I'm happy with you."

"But I'm not happy! You told me recently that something happened to you years ago and yet you won't tell me what." She sniffed and wiped her nose on a tissue.

"That's something different; we're talking about Stuart and Ria."

"But what occurred in the past to make you the way *you* are?" Arla shook her head in frustration.

Toni put down her pen:

"Do you feel up to sharing anything with us, Ric?"

"No; I've never told anybody, and I'm not going to start now. That particular incident is over and done with, and I moved on a long time ago."

"Then we have to abide by Ric's decision, Arla. We have to accept it."

"I'm sick of accepting!" Arla put her head in her hands. "Don't you see? I just know it's the reason behind why he treats his mother like he does – like she's some goddess or something! It's the reason why I came here in the first place! It must be the reason behind why I always feel second best!"

"Give it a rest for God's sake." Ric sighed and folded his arms. "You're letting your imagination run away with you again."

"When Ric's ready then he'll tell you I'm sure." Toni took a sip of water. "Tell me Arla, how do you get on with your own daughter?"

"Okay." Arla sniffed. "We don't see her as much as we'd like though. She lives with her husband and they're self-employed florists. They're always out and about delivering bouquets of flowers and suchlike."

"Are you happy with your son-in-law?"

"Dave treats her well, and they have a good life together. No children yet, but I'm not sure they want any." Arla wondered what Toni's line of questioning was leading up to.

"Did Dave have his own business before he met your daughter, or was it the other way around?" Toni smiled inscrutably.

"No, it was Dave's business. Shelley was out of work, and Dave had put an ad in the newspaper for a shop assistant. He gave Shelley the job, and within six months they had moved in together."

"So in effect, your daughter's original shop assistant post was not too far removed from your daughter-in-law's checkout job?" Toni shrugged.

"I suppose not." Arla sighed. "Stuart's the brains of the family, although Shelley's doing a grand job of running his shop these days."

"So Dave is obviously happy with Shelley as a life partner?" Toni enquired.

"Absolutely. They're very content with each other." Arla replied with some irritation.

"What about Dave's parents? Do they like her?"

"We don't have anything to do with them." Arla could have kicked herself for the revelation, but now had to carry on. "They weren't too pleased when he took up with her."

"Why not?"

"Because Shelley isn't a high-flyer."

Arla wanted to scream louder than she had ever done before in her life; louder even than when she had endured her first roller-coaster ride at the age of ten. Louder than she had screamed during childbirth; loud enough so that she could drown out the whole, mocking world.

CHAPTER 28

"HELLO RICHARD."

She swallowed her anger and smiled sweetly down the phone.

"Hello Edna; it's Arla."

"Oh."

"How are you since having the stent done?"

"Fine thanks."

"I just called to invite you for Sunday lunch."

"Why?"

"No particular reason; Ric was saying the other day that we haven't seen you for a while."

"He knows where I live."

"Well, we've been a bit busy lately."

"Okay then. I can get on the bus; no need to pick me up."

"As you wish. See you about twelve o'clock."

"I'll be there."

As she replaced the receiver Arla exhaled with force, and not for the first time wondered why her mother-in-law had always hated her so much. Was it because she, Arla, had taken away the old woman's last hope for a live-in companion, or had Edna always been of the jealous type and would have hated any girl Ric brought home? Was it because her mother-in-law had decided after their wedding that she felt second place in her son's affections? Had she and Edna ironically been suffering from the same debilitating condition?

She carried on musing and wondering about the intricacies of human relationships as she prepared dinner. There seemed to be no problem with Adie and Ronnie, Edna's two son-in-laws. Both husbands had often been mentioned favourably over the years when they had performed odd jobs for Edna at their wives' request. Arla even remembered Ric once jokingly complaining how he felt redundant regarding the necessity to maintain good upkeep of his mother's house once the son-in-laws had appeared on the scene. Ric had not minded one jot though, and Arla had realised that he was quite happy to let somebody else take over.

She sprinkled some flour on the worktop, rolled out a lump of pastry, and thought back over the counselling sessions as she added some cooked steak and kidney to the dish. She thought about her new daughter-in-law's sunny nature. She came to the conclusion while sticking a pastry leaf on top of the pie that it must definitely be herself who was the weakest link in the chain. All the years of backbiting, jealousy and hatred had caused a rift between her and Ric's family as wide as the English Channel. It was up to her to swallow her pride and try to do something about it.

The pie was steaming and golden brown as she took it out of the oven; perfectly patterned around the edges, and emitting a mouth-watering aroma. She was proud of her culinary creation, but knew an attack with a knife and fork would bring the pie's walls crumbling irretrievably down. She thought about the near thirty year assault on her good name as she set the table, causing her self-confidence to crumble just like the shortcrust pastry. She realised that unless she made the first move to shore up her reputation it would forever be consigned to the rubbish heap, along with the dregs at the bottom of the pie dish.

"Dinner's ready!"

She took a selection of vegetables out of the steamer, and smiled at Ric as he came downstairs glowing from a recent shower.

"That pie smells great."

"It taught me something today."

"What did? The pie?" He broke off the top leaf and ate it.

"Yes; the pie and Ria, and of course Toni. I'm now aware that it *is* me who's the problem. It's up to *me* to set things right. I've invited your mum round for Sunday lunch. I'm going to start straight away." She felt some relief at admitting her shortcomings.

"Good luck with that then." Ric sat down and cut himself a slice of pie.

"Why do you say that?"

"Well, you know what she's like."

"I'm going to make an extra effort."

"Good for you."

However, as she bit into the pie she could not help but experience a small *frisson* of foreboding.

CHAPTER 29

"HELLO EDNA, YOU'RE nice and early!" Arla, flurried, looked up at the clock, which showed twenty minutes past eleven.

"I had to get the quarter to eleven bus; when I phoned to check the times, the bus station people told me the later one had been cancelled."

"No worries; come in and have a cup of tea. Ric's in the shower; he'll be down in a minute."

Edna Deane hung up her coat and looked up and down the hallway.

"You've still got the same wallpaper."

"Well, yes, it's been up a few years, but there's only Ric and myself here now. It doesn't seem to get grubby." Arla's stomach was twisted in knots with nervousness.

"Adie did a good job of decorating my front room last month." Edna sniffed.

"Does he still do that for a living?" Arla prayed for Ric to emerge from the bathroom.

"Yes; you should get him over here to give the place a makeover."

"It's okay; Ric likes to do it himself."

Edna made her way to the kitchen, and Arla followed.

"I'm cooking roast lamb today, and I've made some cheese sauce for your vegetables." Arla felt quite saintly, having reluctantly made several temporary dietary changes that morning in order to curry favour with the old lady.

"Not for me; the doctor says I've got to lay off the cheese now." Edna sniffed again. "Don't pour any on my dinner, whatever you do; it'll clog me up."

Arla sighed and switched on the kettle. The old woman climbed up and sat like an aged Buddha on one of the breakfast bar stools. With what can only be described as ecstatic joy, Arla heard Ric's footsteps on the stairs.

"Hi Mum! If I'd known you were coming over early I'd have had a wash sooner." Ric gave his mother a peck on the cheek. "How are you feeling now?"

"Oh, so-so. The doctor says I've got to cut out pastry, cakes and cheese, and I can only have semi-skimmed milk now. Life's not worth living, is it?"

"Oh, I don't know; Arla hasn't bought full fat milk or cheese for years, and we only eat cake occasionally, but we don't feel deprived. We usually have green tea, but we do eat pastry sometimes. She keeps me fit; I'd weigh twenty stones if it wasn't for her."

"Green tea? I'd rather drink my own piddle." Edna wrinkled her nose in disgust.

"It's okay, Edna; I've bought normal teabags for you."

Arla took a teabag out from a box marked 'Yorkshire Tea', and waved it in front of her mother-in-law's nose. The old lady followed its path towards a mug bearing the epithet 'Best Mum in the World'.

"You can have full-fat milk today if you like; I've bought you some. I won't tell the doctor." Arla chuckled.

"Are you trying to finish me off, then?" Edna's heels kicked at the footrest of the stool.

"Of course not; it'll have to be black tea though; we don't have milk in ours, and I bought the blue cap especially for you." Arla took a deep breath and held the boiling kettle in mid-air over the mug."

"Have some sherry instead, Mum. I take it you still like your mid-morning tipple? Come in the front room and I'll pour you a glass." Ric caught Arla's eye and winked.

"That will be very nice, Richard."

Arla noticed the Buddha's belly undulating as it tried to inch itself off the bar stool with as much dignity as could be mustered for somebody vertically challenged whose feet did not reach the floor.

"I'll get on with the dinner, and let you go in the other room and talk to Ric."

She put her hands together in a prayer-like motion and rolled her eyes to the heavens as she watched Edna shuffling off down the passageway. She turned on the steamer full of vegetables, and checked the roast potatoes' progress in the oven. With a sudden jolt she realised she had been uncharacteristically basting the fat from the meat over the potatoes, and using it to flavour the gravy for Edna's benefit. She decided to say nothing and hope the errors would go unnoticed.

As she was setting the table, she looked up on hearing Ric open the kitchen door:

"The old girl's had two and a half glasses of sherry so far; she's a bit more human now. I daren't give her any more on an empty stomach or she'll be legless." He laughed. "Do you want any help, or shall I just keep Mum out of your way?"

"I'm doing okay; bring her in here at half past twelve."

"She keeps going on about Adie coming round here to do wallpapering."

"That's what she said to me. Our house doesn't need decorating though." Arla looked around.

"Perhaps he hasn't got any work." Ric kissed the top of her head. "See you in a minute, then."

She took much care over the presentation of the lunch, even finding some square plates at the back of the cupboard which somebody had given them for a twenty fifth anniversary present. She chuckled on remembering how Stuart would inform her that sandwiches always tasted better cut on the diagonal, and that food was always somehow more edible if it was set out on square plates. She could hear his voice in her head, and wondered if at the same time as their feast he was tucking into pizza on his lap, as unconcerned as it was possible to be.

"Here we are; Mum, you sit here." Ric patted a chair next to his.

"It all looks very nice, I must say." Edna's mouth managed a faint upward turn.

"Would you like some wine, Edna?" Arla took a bottle out of the fridge.

"Just a little bit; I've already had three glasses of sherry." Edna nodded and speared a potato with her fork.

"It's nice to have you here today." Arla lied through her back teeth and gave the wine to Ric for uncorking.

"Thank you for inviting me. These potatoes taste lovely in olive oil; I remember how you do them. I'll have to try it." Edna chewed appreciatively.

"My mum always told me that the oil slides through your arteries, but fat sticks to them." Arla smiled whilst nearly gagging on the taste of the fatty gravy and salty, lamb-flavoured potatoes.

"Perhaps that's where I went wrong, Richard. If I'd cooked in olive oil then your father might not have dropped down dead in front of you." Edna glugged down a glassful of wine and became misty-eyed. "He died too early, and now *I've* got heart trouble. Keep hold of Arla; you've obviously got a good wife who's been doing her best all these years to keep you alive."

Arla raised her eyebrows and her mouth made a large 'o' of surprise, as she looked at Ric and dropped her fork, which clattered noisily to the floor.

CHAPTER 30

"THE OLD GIRL was out for the count in the car; I think I overdid it with the sherry." Ric closed the front door and hung his car keys up. "Thanks for your efforts with Mum today." He kissed the top of Arla's head.

"Do you think I made an impression?" Arla laughed. "Perhaps she'll tell your sisters what a lovely fat-free dinner she had when she reports in!"

"If that was fat-free I'm a Chinaman." Ric yawned. "Fancy an afternoon nap?"

"Sounds good; I've just finished washing up." Arla took off her apron. "I feel quite sleepy now, too."

"Did you ask about Adie on the way home?" She followed after him up the stairs, and playfully slapped his behind.

"I tried, but she was snoring almost straight away."

They snuggled together fully-clothed on top of the bedcovers. Arla knew she would never be able to sleep unless she asked the question that had been burning in the back of her mind since lunchtime.

"Your mum mentioned something about your dad earlier; that he had dropped down dead in front of you." She let her head sink onto his shoulder. "You've never told me how your dad died."

"It's like Mum said, but I'd rather not talk about it if you don't mind."

His voice had taken on the defensive tone that she had frequently heard in the counselling room. She could hear his rapidly increasing heartbeat, and suddenly she knew that Edna, tongue loosened on three sherries, had inadvertently let the cat out of the bag.

"That's the problem you won't talk about isn't it?" She kept her voice low and slid an arm across his chest.

"There's no problem. The old man's time was up; that's all. He was forty eight, overweight and had a dodgy ticker as it turned out."

"What was he doing when he died?" She held her breath and hoped against hope that he would answer.

"What?"

"What was he doing?"

"Do we have to talk about this?"

"Just once, and then we don't need to mention it again."

He put his arms around her and nuzzled his nose into her hair:

"We were playing football in the garden; nothing too strenuous, just kicking the ball to each other."

She heard his voice change; the bass tone had become husky like an adolescent schoolboy's:

"You blame yourself for his death, don't you?" She closed her eyes, drowning in his heartbeat.

"No, of course I don't; don't be stupid." He swallowed painfully against her forehead.

"You were only young; how old? Eighteen? Nineteen?" She soldiered on, treading on virtual eggshells.

"Eighteen."

"Of course it would affect you at that age!" She held him close. "Ric; you must *not* blame yourself for your father's death!"

"I don't!"

"Yes, you do!"

Nearly three decades of pent up guilt burst like a dam in one giant sob:

"I'm a bastard! If I hadn't been making him run after the ball he might still be alive!" He squeezed her tight and shuddered at the long-hidden memory.

"He had heart disease; he could have died at any time. You were just unlucky enough to witness the outcome of it. There's no way you're to blame; you've got to believe that."

She let him cry into her hair until the thumping of his heart had subsided:

"I'm sure Edna didn't blame you for his death." She whispered and stroked his back.

"Nobody did." His breath came in gulps. "But it was me who had made him run about."

"He probably had a lovely time on his last day on earth, playing football with his son. It's the best way to go actually, don't you think?" She sat up and put his head in her lap. "I'd prefer that any day instead of hanging on by a thread into my nineties and beyond."

"If only I could turn back the clock." He lay still as she stroked his hair.

"Nobody can; we can only move on and learn from the past."

"You should be a bloody counsellor." He sighed and wrapped an arm around her leg.

"You blame yourself for your father's death and for upsetting Edna at the time. Don't you see? It's why you've never said a cross word to her since!"

"She had a terrible shock; just as I did. I'll never forget the look on his face as he fell." He shuddered again. "You're right of course, as you always are; I blamed myself not only for Dad's death, but for causing Mum so much misery. I never want to be in that position again." He relaxed against her and became silent.

As she lay back against the pillows and listened to his deep, regular breathing, she felt as though a huge weight had been lifted off her shoulders. She was light, almost weightless, with relief.

CHAPTER 31

"HELLO?" SHE WAS getting good at this now.

"Hi Arla, it's Ria."

"Hey there! Nice to hear from you!" She smiled.

"I'm just ringing to tell you that we've set a date for the wedding."

"Oh?"

"Yeah; Friday June the twentieth. I won't have too big a bump by then."

"Great! Where?"

"At the Riverside hotel. If we get married on a Friday it keeps the costs down and there's plenty of vacancies. On a Saturday it's twice the price and you have to wait nearly two years."

"Makes sense I suppose." Arla nodded and kept the phone to her ear. "Would you like us to contribute?"

"Mum's paying for all of it, so don't worry about money." Ria's excited voice talked nineteen to the dozen. "Can you come with Mum and me when I buy my dress?"

"Me?"

"Yeah, of course! Why not? You're my mum-in-law aren't you?"

"Well, thank you for asking me. I'd love to come along." Arla grinned. "But isn't it a mother-daughter thing?"

"Mum's trying her best to be interested, but I just know you'll enjoy it more than she will. She's never been much interested in shopping and clothes, bless her."

"I'm looking forward to it already." Arla nodded to nobody in particular.

"See you the Saturday after next. We'll do a tour of bridal shops if you can stand it."

"I'll be at yours about ten; is that okay?"

"Perfect!"

She almost danced up the stairs to Stuart's old bedroom, which was now in use as an office. The monthly chore of invoicing Ric's customers and chasing up late payments did not hold its usual distaste for her that morning. She switched on the computer, and checked her emails whilst waiting for the Sage accounting system to load. There was an address which seemed familiar, yet was not known to her. She opened the email and was surprised by its sender.

'Dear Arla,

I'm sending this around to everybody I know; I've also sent it to Richard amongst hundreds of others, but he has not yet replied.

I wonder if you could have a think and let me know of anybody who might want a room/several rooms or their whole house/outside of the house decorated. What with the recession, Adie's a bit short of work, and we're having to tighten our belts quite a bit. I would be grateful for a reply.

Incidentally, Mum told me what a nice lunch she had at yours the other day. She said she's tried to cook roast potatoes with oil like you do, but she can't seem to make them taste as nice. Perhaps you could let her into your secret?

Hoping to hear from you soon,
Best wishes,
Jan'

Arla mused that as usual it had not taken Edna long to report back to her daughters. As she gathered her paperwork together she railed against the fact that Edna had never called her on the phone to gossip about either Val or Jan's activities, yet the two younger witches of Westen were always readily updated on anything she, Arla, had ever said or done. Her mind drifted and saw the three of them stooped over their usual smoking cauldron; all taking it in turns to stir some more lies about her into the steaming, poisoned pot.

She sighed on realising her negative, jealous thoughts had come to the fore again, as she logged into the first customer's account. She realised that she wanted a better alliance with her own daughter-in-law. The relationship with Edna had always been doomed to fail; her mother-in-law's antagonistic attitude had rubbed her up the wrong way almost from the start, and had left an irreparable mark on her psyche. She realised that unless both parties were willing to make changes, then no mutually respectful bond could ever be formed. She did not know if Edna was too old to change her ways, but she, Arla, could now break the vicious cycle and begin to work on building an agreeable rapport with her son's new wife.

She dithered regarding answering Jan's email; she knew her husband would never entertain the idea of paying his brother-in-law to decorate their house when he could do it himself, and she had no intention of causing Ric any further heartache. Eventually she thought of a suitable response and sat back in the chair to read it through before pressing 'send'.

'Dear Jan,

Thanks for your message. I'll make some flyers this morning with Adie's details on, and will send them out with our monthly invoices. Hopefully one of our customers might be thinking about getting some decorating done.

I'm glad Edna enjoyed her lunch. I always use extra virgin olive oil and a little of the water after par-boiling the potatoes first.

Best wishes,

Arla'

Whilst concentrating on finishing the flyers and month-end figures, she failed to notice one orange-coloured unopened envelope attached to her Outlook icon until the end of the morning.

'Hi Arla,

A thousand thanks for the flyers. They are much appreciated. Love Jan x'

For her sister-in-law to change 'best wishes' to 'love and a kiss' in such a short space of time was no mean feat. Taking into consideration Ria's invitation as well, Arla wondered if Christmas had arrived somewhat earlier than usual.

CHAPTER 32

"I SAW THE difference in the two of you as soon as you walked in!" Toni's smile conveyed genuine warmth.

"We've been getting on so much better. I found out why Ric never wants to upset his mum. It has nothing to do with me, and is due to something that happened a long time ago." Arla sat down and turned to smile at Ric, before holding his hand.

"Blokes find it difficult to talk about things. I haven't said anything to Arla on the way here, but I'd now like to tell you why I've been a complete prat all these years." Ric looked at Toni and sighed.

"That's wonderful, Ric. In your own time though, and only when you're ready." Toni opened her notebook and picked up a pen.

"I was a teenager. All boys look up to their dads don't they? I was proud of my old man; he was a train driver. As I told you before, he would take what little spare time he had to take me to football matches or show me how to change the oil in the car and so on." Ric took a sip of water and looked down at the carpet. "We were kicking a football around in the garden one Sunday afternoon, when he dropped down dead in front of me."

"Goodness; what an ordeal for a young boy to have to go through!" Toni looked sympathetically at Ric, who gave a wry smile.

"I've never forgotten it."

"Well of course you wouldn't. Who would?" Toni agreed.

"I stood there rooted to the spot, watching him dying and gasping for breath. His face turned blue. My legs went to jelly and I couldn't move with the shock of it." Ric coughed. "I wasn't even aware that piss was running down the inside of my trousers until later."

Arla moved closer to Ric, and clasped his right hand with both of her own:

"Not many people ever have to go through something like this." She kissed his knuckles.

"Indeed." Toni nodded. "Did you ever have counselling afterwards?"

"No; it was years ago; I was only eighteen. I was a baby really; counselling was never suggested, and I wouldn't have gone anyway." Ric sniffed and shrugged.

"How did your dad's death affect you?" Toni looked interrogatively at Ric.

"I felt it was my fault he'd died. If I hadn't made him run around in the garden, then I knew that probably he might still be alive. It caused so much misery for Mum, and for years afterwards I couldn't bear to see her unhappy again. I just carried on trying to make her life easier by not upsetting her. It became a habit. I still can't break it now." He wiped away a tear and exhaled shakily. "Mum had saved me from getting a police record, and as far as I was concerned I repaid her by killing her husband."

Toni passed Ric a tissue:

"Was there an autopsy performed on the body?"

"Yeah. The outcome was that his heart was diseased and he could have gone at any time." Ric blew his nose.

"So you realise now with the advantage of maturity how it was no fault of your own that your father died?" Toni nodded for emphasis.

"Sure, but it's taken years of fighting with my conscience to accept it."

"You must accept it, Ric, for your own peace of mind." Arla gave his arm a squeeze.

"I'm getting there, but it's difficult to break the habit of a lifetime."

"Val and Jan must have their own reasons for not making your mum upset." Arla wondered aloud.

"Yeah, I suppose so. Mum didn't want Val to marry Ronnie and they had some terrible rows. Perhaps Val was fed up with all the arguments. As for Jan, who knows? Mum always got on well with Adie." Ric shrugged.

"You've got bits of tissue on your stubble." Arla picked them off.

"Bollocks to it." Ric gave a wry laugh and sighed.

"Arla, how did you feel when Ric told you his story?" Toni switched her interest.

"Relief really for two reasons; one that he'd finally got it off his chest, and two, satisfaction in knowing that all my fears about being second best to his mother were untrue." Arla smiled. "But there's also the guilt there that I've caused Ric so much anguish because of my jealous nature."

"You're not second best; I've always told you that." Ric shook his head.

"I now understand the reasons why you treat her the way you do."

"She's a difficult old lady, I know. She says things she shouldn't, but at the end of the day she's my mum. I'd never hurt the old girl, but I love you more. Mum's had a hard time of it, and my reasons are different now; I don't want to make her miserable in the last few years of her life."

"I'll never mention it again, but Ric, do you think I'm a hard, jealous bitch?" Arla looked at her husband and wanted to crawl into the woodwork with shame.

"I love you; I've always loved you. I'll love you until they put the last nail in my coffin. Sure, sometimes I've seen a bit of jealousy there, but my mum and sisters are difficult people to get along with. You're trying to change with Ria, and I'm proud of you." Ric reached over to give Arla a kiss.

Toni closed her notebook:

"It's wonderful to counsel couples who can resolve their issues and are able to forgive each other. It's total job satisfaction for me. You see, it's only with forgiveness that you can both move forward in your relationship. You'll never forget what's happened in the past, but I can tell that you're both willing to let bygones be bygones. Good luck to both of you."

Arla stood up, followed by Ric:

"Thanks so much for your help Toni." She fished in her purse. "I've enjoyed our sessions."

"This one's on me; it's great to see the pair of you so happy."

As she walked out of the door, Arla felt as though she was floating on air.

"Counselling *did* help us, didn't it?" She gave Ric a peck on the cheek as they walked towards the car.

"Yeah; you were right as usual. Sorry I gave you such a hard time about it." Ric squeezed her hand. "It's hard for us blokes to talk about what's bothering us."

"I know; you're much too macho to talk." Arla giggled. "You can just grunt from now on if you like."

"What – like a caveman?" Ric let go of her hand and thumped his chest. "I'll gather you up and take you off to my cave if you like."

"Your man cave? No thanks." Arla laughed. "It would be too, too scary."

CHAPTER 33

"HI RIA! Hi Mandy, it's good to see you both again!" Arla hugged both women on the doorstep.

"You're in luck this morning; your son's at home as well!" Ria returned the hug.

"I can see him coming down the stairs." Arla laughed and looked over Ria's shoulder. "He looks like death on legs."

"Late gig last night." Stuart yawned. "Hello Mum. Come in and make me a cup of coffee."

"On your bike." Arla punched him playfully on the arm.

"Are you ready for the wedding dress dash today?" Mandy looked at Arla and grinned.

"Absolutely. We'll have to think of a collective noun for them."

"A rustle? A fluttering? A meringue?" Mandy winked.

"I'm not wearing any meringue." Ria shook her head. "No, more like a whispering of wedding dresses; all that silk, chiffon and tulle. I can't wait!"

"My purse is feeling the strain already." Mandy's mouth turned down at the corners.

"Stu's going to give us a lift into town, and then pick us up later on." Ria nodded to Arla.

"Is he up to it?

"I'll be alright once I've had a coffee. Talk amongst yourselves and I'll be ready in ten minutes." Stuart yawned again and headed for the kitchen.

Oxford Street was heaving with shoppers as Arla waved goodbye to Stuart and stood blinking on the pavement with the others, taking a moment to adjust to the brightly-lit shops, hooting traffic, and surging crowds.

"I've done my homework; I've booked slots in Selfridges, House of Fraser, Debenhams, and The Bridal Room." Ria looked up and down the street. "But first of all I need a wee."

"Yep; I remember it well." Arla laughed. "Ric used to get annoyed when I was pregnant. Everywhere we went in the car we had to keep stopping."

"The first one's Debenhams isn't it, Ria? Come on; there'll be toilets in there." Mandy took charge. "It's this way; not far from Bond Street tube."

Agile despite her girth, Mandy began to take long strides. Late spring had started to give way to early summer, and Arla was perspiring by the time they reached the cool interior of the store.

"I'll see you in the wedding section in a minute; I'm off to the loo." Ria made her way to the escalator.

"I'll come with you." Mandy followed behind.

Arla sat down and rested her legs. She could see several prospective brides and their proud mothers already ensconced amongst the frills and fripperies. The younger women's faces were suffused with wonder, and the older ones smiled with a kind of world-weariness. Thinking back to her own wedding preparations, Arla smiled to herself as she recalled arguing about her mother's choice of dress, complaining how she would resemble a caricature of Little Bo Peep.

"We're back! Which one shall I try on first?" Ria scanned the racks under the beady eye of a shop assistant.

"Don't forget to leave room for expansion; you'd have grown a bit more in another month." Mandy instructed.

"White or ivory?" Arla stood up again and hoped for the latter.

"Oh, it's got to be ivory I suppose; hardly anybody's a virgin on their wedding night these days are they?" Ria shrugged.

"You're right there; we moved in together first too. I always told my two to live with somebody before getting married; at least you know what you're letting yourself in for." Arla nodded.

"Yeah, you could be marrying the biggest perv on the planet." Ria laughed and pulled out a dress. "What do you think of this one?"

"Actually, I was." Mandy held her hand up.

"Was what? A perv?" Ria put the dress up against her.

"No! A virgin on my wedding night."

"Really? Wow!" Ria looked at her mother with interest. "I never knew that!"

"It's not the sort of thing you go round telling everybody. The dress is meringue-like. Have another look." Mandy shook her head.

"I just finished reading a book about a perv called The Porn Detective. She was a virgin on her wedding night as well." Arla chuckled. "Poor cow. The story's partly true as well. The husband was into porn in a big way and she never found out for thirty years; he had managed to hide a completely different part of his personality from her."

"Blimey; I'll have to read that one." Ria replied.

Arla could not help but notice a common denominator.

"Why don't the majority of these dresses have any tops to them?"

"No-one wants to be done up like Little Miss Muffett anymore. If you've got it, flaunt it." Ria stuck out her chest and giggled.

"You've definitely got it, girl." Mandy nodded. "But do we all want to see it?"

"Stu does." Ria chuckled.

"Too much information there." Arla put her hands over her ears.

"What about this one?" Mandy pulled out a more decorous silkier design with looser lines and a flimsy bolero.

"I like that." Arla smiled. "It will suit you, Ria."

"I'm not sure about the little cardigan thing."

"It's not a cardigan, it's called a bolero." Mandy rolled her eyes to the heavens.

"No; a bolero is a dance, like the Torvill and Dean thing." Ria shook her head. "They showed it on TV again last week."

"It's a jacket and a dance." Arla laughed.

"Explain that to the foreigners. Okay, I'll try it on."

When Ria stepped out of the changing room, Arla was surprised to see tears in Mandy's eyes.

"You look beautiful!" Mandy sniffed and reached for a tissue.

"Don't worry; all the mothers do it." The shop assistant nodded.

"I'm not usually the crying type." Mandy wiped her eyes. "I don't know what's come over me."

"We've still got another three shops to do; your mascara will be a mess at the end of the day!" Ria twirled and held the dress out for inspection.

"I feel like crying as well, now." Arla's voice broke. "I can see now that my son's a very lucky man."

"Oh Arla, what a lovely thing to say! Thank you!" Ria's eyes began to water.

As the shop assistant handed round a box of tissues, Arla, Ria and Mandy wiped their eyes and burst into peals of laughter.

CHAPTER 34

THE LITTLE STREAM that meandered along at the back of the Riverside Hotel was swollen with the previous night's rain. Arla's heels dug into the soft grass as she and Ric mingled amongst hungry guests waiting to be ushered into the marquee nearby for a sumptuous wedding breakfast.

"So, Ric, we meet at last!" Mandy laughed. "I probably guessed correctly that you weren't too keen on traipsing around Oxford Street with us looking for dresses."

"Err.. yeah, something like that." Ric loosened his tie. "It's not really me."

"Especially after Ria dragged us around every wedding shop and then chose the dress she originally tried on in the first place!" Arla linked her arm through Ric's. "She looks lovely today though, so it was well worth it."

"Thank you; my daughter *is* radiant today."

"What did you think of the service?" Arla looked questioningly at Mandy. "I'm used to weddings being in a church, but then again I'm old-fashioned I suppose."

"Ria's not religious, and I guess neither is Stuart. It makes sense for them to have had it here. It's what they wanted; I'm just paying for it all." Mandy shrugged.

Arla accepted a strawberry and a glass of champagne from one of the peripatetic waitresses, and smiled at Jan and Adie, who came towards them.

"Thanks for sending out those flyers. A couple of your customers replied; Adie's got some work lined up now." Jan beamed and held her husband's hand.

"That's great news! I'm glad I was able to help."

"Appreciate it." Adie seemed pleased but uncomfortable.

As Jan and Adie wandered away again, Arla turned and looked at Ric in surprise:

"Jan's talking to me now!"

"It just goes to show, doesn't it?" Ric signalled with one hand. "Hey Adie!"

"What?" Adie turned back towards them.

"Can you give me a quote for painting the outside of our house?"

"Sure!" Adie grinned. "I'll give you mates' rates!"

"Yeah; you'd better do." Ric chuckled.

The bridegroom, resplendent in a pale grey morning suit, crisp white shirt and pink cravat, made his way across the lawn.

"Mum; Dad, the photographer wants you to pose."

"Oh, not again." Ric *tutted* with irritation. "My jaw aches from smiling."

"Force yourself, you miserable old git." Arla elbowed him in the chest.

With some dismay she found herself standing next to Val and Edna in the line-up:

"Hello Edna; enjoying the day?" Arla struggled to think of something pleasant to say.

"I will when I can sit down." Edna could not conceal a pained expression on her face.

"I'll go and ask if I can take you inside early." Val held out her arm. "Hold on, Mum."

"Hi Val; I'm sure we'll be able to go in soon. Shall I ask the waiter to bring a chair out in the meantime?" Arla smiled and tried to make eye contact.

Silence.

Oh well, you can't win them all. Arla ignored the snub and linked her arm through Ric's again.

"Arla just asked you a question, Val." Ric looked sideways past Arla towards his sister.

"Did she?" Val kept her eyes on the photographer. "Well

I heard her anyway, and I'm sure you must have done, unless you're deaf." Ric squeezed Arla's arm and gave her a wink. "But then you *are* getting on a bit. Actually, yeah, you're probably as deaf as a bloody post."

"Richard!" Val looked shocked at her brother's outburst. "Ronnie, you can't let him speak to me like that!"

"And Ric's the name for Christ's sake; don't ever call me Richard again." Ric, ignoring his mother, stared out both Val and Ronnie.

"Fuck you." Val's eyes lowered and filled with tears.

"Yeah, go off and fuck yourself." Ronnie sneered at Ric, but was the first to lower his eyes.

Arla's triumphant grin was genuine for the photographer. When the snap was taken and Val and Ronnie had stormed off in high dudgeon, Ric signalled to the waiter to bring out a chair. As Edna slumped down in relief, she remained uncharacteristically silent.

"Sorry about that little argument, Mum. I'm fed up with Val refusing to speak to Arla for no apparent reason." Ric put an arm around his mother's shoulders, who sighed and suddenly appeared to Arla to have aged.

"It's okay; my knees are killing me too much to bother about it anyway. One thing I've just learned though; I never knew you preferred to be called Ric." "I've always preferred Ric."

"Well, why haven't you said anything about it before?" Edna looked up at her son.

"Oh, I don't know." Ric shrugged.

"He never wanted to rock the boat." Arla interjected. "But he'd be really pleased if you'd call him Ric from now on."

"I will, then." Edna smiled weakly. "Arla, I'm sorry if I've been a bit of a cow to you over the years. I'm getting old and crotchety, and after sitting through that lovely wedding service I've started to realise that families must stick together in the long run."

"That's alright, Edna. Apology accepted. I think they're calling us in now."

Arla smiled at Ric as she helped her mother-in-law to get to her feet, and decided that after nearly thirty years, to get two out of three witches on her side was not bad going at all.

"Thanks darling, for sticking up for me." She whispered over Edna's head.

"My chuffing pleasure. It's about time Val had a taste of her own medicine."

She let Ric escort Edna into the marquee, hanging back to find her own mother in the queue.

"Edna's just apologised for being a cow to me all these years!"

"Good God!" Irene Fenton nearly dropped her champagne glass. "Get it in writing before she changes her mind!"

As she sat down for the wedding breakfast Arla grinned to nobody in particular, and felt a wave of happiness wash over her that was not entirely due to the marriage of her son.

"Happy?" Ric turned his head to look at her and smiled.

"Yes; happy." Arla's face was beaming as she returned his smile.

CHAPTER 35

SHE LIFTED UP the receiver, looking forward to a possible girly chat.

"Hello."

"Hello Arla, it's Ria."

"Hey! How's my grandchild cooking?"

"Not long to go now. I'm starting to get uncomfortable."

"You will do I'm afraid." Arla sympathised.

"I'd like to ask you a question if I may." Ria's voice sounded more serious than usual.

"Sure; go ahead."

There was a hint of hesitation, but then Ria sounded more like her old self.

"Would you consider being my birth partner please?"

"Me?" Arla sat down in surprise on a nearby chair. "Yes.

It's like this; you know how squeamish Stuart is, well he now tells me that he's changed his mind and just wants to wait outside. Adding to that, although Mum's a doctor, she opted for psychiatry because she was always more interested in the mind than the body, and can't stand blood, guts and vomit. She even paid for a planned caesarean when I was due."

"Oh." Arla tried to keep a straight face. "Of course I will. I'm not squeamish in the least after my seven years as a nurse, also I've had two natural births and two accident-prone kids. You don't want to be in the labour room with a load of strangers for your first delivery."

"Thanks so much! I *was* hoping you'd say yes." Ria's voice told of her obvious relief. "We've got a spare bedroom; come and stay for the last week or so. You'll be able to look around the labour ward with me as well."

"Sure; I'll help in any way I can." Arla smiled down the phone. "I take it that Stuart is going with you to all your ante-natal classes?"

"Yes he is, but he messes about though. The other night we were all sitting in a circle preparing to practise our breathing, when he asked if all the blokes were going to throw their keys in the middle. You should have seen the midwife's face."

"That sounds like my son!" Arla burst out laughing.

"He's not taking it seriously at all."

"Don't worry; he will when the baby's here."

"Well, I've got to go because of another hospital appointment now. The baby's due on October the twentieth, so if you come the day before, that'll be a Sunday and you can stay."

"Lovely! Don't worry; I'll be there."

Arla replaced the receiver with a smile. She thought back to her own time in the labour ward; she would never have envisaged ever asking her own mother-in-law to be a birth partner. She remembered how Ric had seen his two children come into the world, and how the experience had strengthened the bond between them. She closed her eyes briefly to bring back the mental image of her tearful and exhausted husband holding up their new-born daughter, still covered in her protective vernix. She had a sudden idea to phone Stuart straight away to try and get him to change his mind, but then recalled Toni's advice about not interfering with others' choices. She pulled her hand away from the phone with a sigh.

She was still musing on her daughter-in-law's request when she heard Ric's van pulling up on the driveway at the end of the afternoon. She stood on the doorstep to welcome him, wrapping her cardigan more securely around her to ward off the early October chill.

"Hello darling; good day?" She kissed him. "You need a shave."

"Give us a chance; I've just got in!" He replied good-naturedly. "Busy day, but good."

"Me too; I had a phone call from Ria this morning; she wants me to be her birth partner."

"Ewwww! What about Stuart? Shouldn't *he* be there?" Ric hung up his jacket.

"He's chickened out."

"No surprise there then."

"And you're okay with it? I remember from my end it was pretty gory stuff." He chuckled and went into the kitchen. "What's for dinner? I'm starving."

She followed behind him and turned off the oven.

"They gave me a mirror, remember? And it's pizza tonight."

"Pizza? We never have pizza!"

"Get a load of this then." She opened the oven door. "You seemed to enjoy it when Ria served it up, so I asked the supermarket girl to make one up specially. It's got pepperoni on it, and broccoli and sweetcorn as well, so at least you'll be getting two types of veg today."

"It looks like Stuart's face did when he was about fourteen." Ric looked at it approvingly.

"Don't be mean. And I've done oven chips so you don't get a heart attack." Arla took out a second tray.

"Cheers for that." Ric took a chip off the tray. "Can't you deep fry them just for once?"

"Bugger off. Be grateful for what you've got."

"I *am* grateful." He kissed her forehead. "You're the best thing that's ever happened to me."

She sat down and served up the pizza, and was surprised to discover that it really *was* rather tasty.

CHAPTER 36

"OH RIA, I love the stencils! Did you do them yourself?" Arla looked appreciatively around the nursery at several Winnie-the-Poohs and Eeyores.

"Yes, I've always been quite arty." Ria nodded. "Dad and I often sat down to draw or paint together."

"I wish I could have done something like that for my two." Arla looked up. "Who did the moon and the stars on the ceiling?"

"All my own work; I did it before I got too big."

"How many days overdue are you now?"

"Three, but the midwife's happy to leave it a few more, as my blood pressure is okay."

"Lucky you; I was laid up for a month before Shelley was born and then I had to be induced in the end."

"I'm hoping it'll start soon; I'm really cheesed off now."

"You know the best way to get it all moving, don't you?" Arla kept a straight face.

"What?"

"Jump on Stuart tonight in bed."

"How can I with you lying there in the next room?"

"Easy; just tell me when you're going to do it and I'll put my headphones on. I've got three hundred tunes on my iPod; that should be enough time I reckon."

"Jeez; I'm not sure if I'll even need one song at the moment!"

"I've got a long song, *Bohemian Rhapsody,* I'll turn it up loud."

They were giggling like two schoolgirls as Stuart came out of the bathroom, fresh from a shower.

"What are you two laughing about?"

"Girl talk." Arla kissed her son. "Night night; I'm going to bed now. I've got all my clothes ready to put on in case baby starts to make an appearance." She kissed Ria. "Goodnight daughter-in-law; remember what I said."

"What did you say?" Ria's eyes twinkled.

"I said I feel like listening to *Bohemian Rhapsody.*"

Arla smiled, closed the door to the spare bedroom, and took off her dressing gown. She was not especially sleepy; the single bed was unfamiliar, and she wondered if it was going to be one of those times when she laid awake all night. She wished she had remembered to bring her memory foam pillow; Stuart and Ria were doing their best, but as she slipped between the sheets she came to the conclusion that there was nothing like the comfort of your own bed.

She must have dozed into a fitful sleep, because the next thing she knew her son's voice was insistent in her ear. She struggled back to consciousness to see Stuart standing over her fully-dressed, and the digital clock displaying two twenty three in a still-darkened room:

"Mum; here's a cup of tea. Ria thinks the baby has started."

"Oh!" She sat up. "Give me five minutes to drink this and get my clothes on, and I'll be ready."

Behind her son she could see that Ria had come into the room.

"Sorry to wake you, Arla, but my waters have broken; the bed's soaking wet."

"The baby's definitely on its way then." Arla glugged down her tea. "Are you having any contractions yet?"

"I can feel something happening. It's like a band around my middle that gets tighter and tighter and then stops." Ria nodded.

"Yep; sounds good. Okay; get your things together and I'll just clean my teeth and get dressed. As far as I can remember from my own experience without going into too much gory detail, it's probably best that you don't have a lot to eat, but just nibble on some crackers or something to keep your blood sugar up. Stuart, is the car's windscreen icy?"

"I'll have a look and sort it out."

"Ria, have you phoned the hospital?"

"Yes; just now. They told me to come in. I've phoned Mum as well; she's going to wait with Stuart."

"Will you want any pain relief when you get there?"

"No; I want a natural birth."

Arla thought Stuart seemed pleased to be able to do something. She dressed quickly, found some plain biscuits in the kitchen, and put them in her handbag before following Stuart and Ria out of the front door and into the car.

"The tightening feeling's getting a bit painful now." Ria looked over her shoulder at Arla in the back seat with something akin to panic.

"It will do; it's a sign that things are underway. I know it's hard to do, but try and take some deep breaths when you get the sensation and concentrate your mind on something else, for instance an object you can see." Arla remembered the raw pain of childbirth, and was reluctant to inform the mother-to-be that this was only the beginning.

"I'll try and avoid all the bumps in the road." Stuart pulled away slowly from the kerb.

The rest of the short journey was carried out in silence, apart from a few winces of discomfort coming from the front passenger seat. At the hospital Arla helped Ria out of the car and into a wheelchair, whilst Stuart drove off to find a parking space.

"I'll wheel you upstairs to the labour ward now. Let's go and find the lift."

"I want to go home, Arla."

"You will, love, as soon as the baby's born."

Arla could hear that Ria sounded like a frightened little girl. She pressed the button for the lift, anxious to share her precious cargo with the professional midwives on the labour ward. Arriving at Reception she waited for Ria to announce herself to the waiting nurse, but the mother-to-be was doubled over in pain in the wheelchair.

"This is my daughter-in-law, Ria Deane. She phoned earlier; her waters have broken and the contractions are coming about every ten minutes. I'm her birth partner, Arla Deane."

"Ah, yes; Mrs Deane. I'm Letty; I remember you came with Ria a couple of weeks ago to look around the labour ward. I'll show you to your room. Is the father attending?"

"No; he'll be waiting outside with Ria's

mother." "Come this way."

Arla recognised the same room that she had seen before. After helping a silent Ria into a hospital gown, Letty reappeared.

"Mrs Deane; I just need to ask you to wait outside while we examine Ria, and then you can come back in."

"Okay; Ria, I'll just be outside for a minute."

"Don't go away." Ria's voice trembled. "I won't."

Arla took a sip of water from the drinking fountain and shared a dry biscuit with her son when he appeared.

"They're just examining her now; I have to wait out here."

"Thanks so much for this, Mum; I can't do it." Stuart exhaled slowly. "Mandy's just phoned me; she's parking the car now. I've sent Dad a text, but he'll be asleep now."

"Yes, he'll be out cold, but at least you'll have some company with Mandy here as well; I'll call you in when the gory bit's over."

"Love you, Mum." Stuart smiled weakly.

"Love you too."

CHAPTER 37

AFTER SIX HOURS of pacing the confines of the labour room with Ria, Arla was becoming rather weary, but found her daughter-in-law's resolve not to take painkilling drugs quite remarkable.

"You're doing so well, Ria. I was definitely asking for Pethidine or gas and air by now." Arla gave a supporting hug, and was rewarded with a smile.

"Once I've made up my mind, I tend to stick it out. I want to do it my way."

"Of course you do; you're doing fantastic. How about a warm bath?"

"No; I want to stay upright." Ria winced as another contraction came.

"You'll have to get on the bed when you want to push; you know that."

"Yes, but until then I'm going to hobble about with my glucose drip; it's the new fashion accessory." Ria winced, suddenly clutching the drip stand and stooping over. "I feel sick."

"I'll call Letty in; it probably means the birth is not too far away now. That's why I suggested you don't eat much." Arla pressed the call button.

"There's nothing to come up; I last ate nearly twelve hours ago now." Ria moaned with pain and retched. "Sorry; I can't help it."

"What's going on? Mrs Deane, you'll be better on the bed now." Letty cast a professional eye over the patient. "Come on; I'll lower the bed and you won't have to climb up."

"I'm frightened!" Ria clutched the drip stand as though her life depended on it.

"You're not ill; you're having a baby, and you're doing wonderfully. The baby is in a good position. I'm sure it'll all be over soon." Letty guided her patient towards the bed.

"I'm here with you, Ria. Don't worry." Arla tried to voice her most soothing tones. "We're going to bring this baby into the world together."

"I want Stu! I want to go home!" Ria screamed with pain. "I'm going to be sick!"

Letty quickly produced a kidney bowl. "I

need to check how far you're dilated."

"Arla! Don't go away!" Ria retched, eyes wild with pain and fear.

"I'm here, Ria. Concentrate on my face while Letty examines you. Look at me."

Arla stared into the frightened woman's eyes and held her hand.

"What colour eyes have I got, Ria?" Arla stopped herself from blinking.

"Brown." Ria's retching ceased, and she sobbed and stared.

"You are nearly fully dilated. You'll soon feel the need to push as though you want to open your bowels." Letty stood up. "I would think within the next half an hour."

Arla could see the paling of the sky outside:

"It's the twenty fourth of October today; your child's birthday."

"If it ever comes." Ria shuddered with pain. "Oh, God I want to push." She sat up, bent her legs, and clutched her knees.

"I'll call Letty in; just for now don't push, Ria. Don't push, just in case you're not fully dilated." Arla pressed the call button again.

"I can't help it; I've got to." Ria panted to try and stem the sensation.

Letty came into the room, followed by another, younger woman.

"This is Angie, a trainee midwife. Are you happy for her to watch the birth?" Letty smiled at Ria.

"I just want this baby out! I don't care who watches!" Perspiring, Ria took a deep breath and pushed.

"Let me have a look." Letty examined Ria's abdomen and perineum. "Yes, you're fully dilated; push again when you have the next pain. This is the labouring bit; you've got to do some hard work now."

"The baby's almost here, Ria! You're doing really well!" Arla gently dragged back Ria's wet hair from her forehead.

"Yes, the perineum's bulging, and I can see the head starting to present in the birth canal!" Letty smiled. "Come on Mrs Deane, push for England! Push out through your bottom when you get the next contraction!"

Pleased at being able to do something productive, Ria grabbed a better hold of her knees, took another deep breath, closed her eyes, and pushed with all her might.

"That's it, Ria! The head's coming out!" Arla was beside herself with joy. "Ria; I can see the head!"

Ria, drenched in sweat, was lost in her own bodily sensations. Uttering a kind of animalistic, guttural growl, she pushed until she could push no more.

"That's it! The head's out, Ria! It's nearly over!" Arla felt tears stinging her eyes at the sight of her grandchild's wet head. "The baby's got dark hair, just like you!"

"Would you like a mirror to see?" Letty gave a mirror to Arla. "Just say, and your mother-in-law will hold it out for you."

There was no reply from Ria, silent whilst concentrating on aiding the baby's passage from her body. Arla placed the mirror on the bedside cabinet.

"Give one more push Mrs Deane, and you'll have your baby."

Arla watched as Ria gave a beatific smile, came back to the present, and pushed her baby out into the cold, unforgiving world.

"It's a boy, Ria. You've got a little boy!" Arla sobbed and kissed Ria's cheek, who fell back weakly against the pillows.

"Let me see him!" Ria cried with relief.

"Letty's going to cut the cord. She'll give him to you in a moment." Arla watched the now business-like midwives at work.

"I just need to give you a little injection in your thigh first, Ria, to make sure the placenta comes away nicely." Letty smiled and picked up a syringe.

Ria gave no indication that she was aware of the injection at all, and Arla saw Letty supervise Angie as the trainee midwife expertly clamped the now decreasingly pulsating umbilical cord and wrapped the baby in a towel. Ria held out her arms, already the natural mother she always wanted to be.

"Can Stu come in now?" Ria's tears fell unashamedly.

"We need to deliver the afterbirth first." Letty was suddenly business-like. "I'm going to push down on your abdomen; give me a little cough."

Arla was relieved her son was still waiting outside as her grandson's lifeline for the previous nine months fell out into a dish. Hot, exhausted, and bedraggled with sweat, she sank down into an armchair.

"Thanks so much, Arla, for your help. You've been an absolute brick." Ria cuddled her son. "I'll never forget all you've done for me."

"My pleasure; a birth is truly a miracle. I'll call Stuart in, and your mum?" Arla wiped her eyes.

"He'd prefer it if you called him Stu." Ria nodded and yawned.

"Really?"

"Yeah; he hates being called Stuart."

"I never knew that." Arla felt genuine surprise.

"Honestly; he does, but come here and hold your grandson first. You deserve it. "

Arla felt the warm little bundle in her arms and sobbed:

"What's his name? He's beautiful!" Her breath came in hiccups.

"We decided on Jon David; I've got every one of Jon Bon Jovi's albums."

"Good thing you're not a fan of Marilyn Manson then!" Arla laughed through her tears, kissed her grandson's forehead, and then handed him back to his proud mother.

CHAPTER 38

"THEY WANT ME to stay one more day to help out. I offered to go home, but Ria said no. Her mum has clinics, and Stu…we have to call him Stu now…is a bit overwhelmed." Arla sat on her son's spare bed with her mobile phone to her ear and chuckled.

"Stu?"

"Yeah; apparently that's what he prefers."

"I'll come down tomorrow and pick you up." Ric gave a wry laugh. "Stu; you're right, it definitely *does* sound like a casserole."

"I've had a nice shower and a sleep; Stuart's bringing Ria and the baby home today." Arla fished around on the floor for her slippers.

"Stu, don't forget." Ric guffawed.

"Oh yeah." Arla yawned and looked at the clock. "They'll be here soon, and I'm not awake properly yet."

"You will be when that baby starts up." Ric chuckled. "I've missed you; look forward to seeing you again."

"That's nice to hear. I've missed you too." Arla blew him a kiss. "Did you hear that?"

"What? Did you fart?"

"I'm going to ignore that and get ready to cuddle my grandson. Bye bye."

She was dressed and eating some beans on toast when a key turned in the lock.

"Hi Mum; we're back!"

"Hey Stua....Stu!" She finished the last mouthful, took a gulp of tea, and stood up.

"I'll go and get more stuff from the car." Stuart gave a wave and disappeared.

Ria, looking pale and tired, walked in slowly carrying the baby.

"Hey daughter-in-law! How's it going?" Arla gave her a grin.

"I don't know yet. I don't know what day it is either. All I know is that I want to sleep." Ria smiled weakly.

"Go and sit down in the front room. There's already some tea in the pot; I'll pour you a cup."

"Thanks; I'm absolutely shattered."

"You will be for quite a few days I'm afraid; childbirth takes it out of you."

"Would you like to hold Jon?" Ria laid down on the settee "He'll be due for a feed soon. I'm breastfeeding, so have a nice cuddle while it lasts."

"Lovely! I learned to do everything one-handed years ago while holding a baby; let's see if I've lost the knack."

Arla took the baby and went into the kitchen. By the time she returned with a cup of tea, Ria was asleep. Stuart took the cup from her as she sat with the baby in an armchair.

"He's so tiny! What do I do with him if he cries?" Stuart sipped some tea and looked over at her helplessly.

"You'll soon learn; don't worry." Arla stroked the tiny unlined brow and felt a warm glow of fulfilment.

"Aunty Val rang my mobile; she wanted to bring Granny round this afternoon to see the baby."

"Isn't that a bit too soon? What did you say?" Arla looked up at him.

"I couldn't say no really." Stuart shrugged.

"Oh, gawd. That's going to be fun." Arla rolled her eyes. "Val hasn't spoken to me for ages; long before your wedding."

"Well, we'll have to do something about that, won't we?" Ria yawned and sat up.

"I thought you were asleep." Arla smiled.

"How can I with you two nattering away? Tell you what; I'll feed and change Jon, and then I'll go up to bed for an hour or so until they get here."

"Okay; we can hold the fort, can't we Stu?" Arla felt strange uttering the abbreviation.

"Er……..sure…" Stuart laughed.

Arla decided to take the opportunity to speak candidly to her son when Ria had left the room.

"I'm sorry if I initially gave the impression that I didn't like Ria." Arla inwardly winced with shame.

"That's alright, Mum. She doesn't always come over favourably to start with; she's usually nervous at meeting people for the first time."

"She's a lovely girl; your children will be well looked after."

"I know; that's one of the reasons I chose her. If I had married a career girl then we would have had to pay for somebody to look after them. A career wife would not have been happy to stay home all day, but it's all Ria wants."

"You're a lucky man, and very perceptive if I may say so."

"Well, I have got letters after my name now." Stuart grinned.

"I always said to Dad that you were the brains of the family."

"Cheers!"

I've found out a few things about myself over the last few months; not all of them pleasant." Arla sighed. "

"Don't be so hard on yourself." Stuart looked at her. "You're fine, Mum; honestly."

"There you go, just like your father; telling me what you think I want to hear."

"No, I'd never do that." Stuart shook his head. "We've always been able to speak our minds plainly. If I had a problem with something you'd said, you would be the first one to hear about it."

"Well, that's a relief anyway!"

Chuckling, pleasingly relaxed, and cuddling the baby whilst enjoying the chat with Stuart, Arla's heart sank when she heard the doorbell's chimes. She heard Ria come downstairs and join Stuart at the front door as he welcomed the visitors, but stayed put in the comfortable armchair gazing down at the little face which already seemed to show a marked resemblance to her son.

"What are *you* doing here?" Val breezed into the room, glanced at Arla, and then took off her coat and flung it onto a chair.

"Arla's staying here until tomorrow; she's been a tower of strength to me." Ria followed in close behind Val.

"Hello Edna; you've got a lovely great-grandson." Arla smiled at her mother-in-law, ignored Val, and clutched the baby tighter to her chest.

"Hello Arla." Edna replied. "Stuart phoned yesterday to tell me the good news."

"Mum would like to hold the baby." Val stood menacingly in front of Arla and held out her arms.

"Leave him for now; you'll wake him up. He's quite comfortable where he is." Ria defused the situation with ease. "Would you like tea or coffee Val?"

"Tea please." Val shot Arla an intimidatory stare, before stomping back to sit next to her mother on the settee.

"And you, Edna?"

"Coffee, thanks."

"I'll do it." Stuart held up one hand. "You sit down, Ria, and I'll bring some drinks in."

Ria's quick wink was not lost on Arla, who lowered her eyes towards the baby whilst keeping her face expressionless. At that precise moment her grandson chose to regain consciousness, and gazed balefully at her before screwing his face up and letting out a mighty howl. Arla stood up with him and began pacing the room, aware that Val was following her every move.

"He's probably hungry; you'll need to give him back to Ria." Val spoke to Arla through virtually gritted teeth.

"He hasn't long been fed, actually. "Ria smiled. "I'll tell you what…."

"What?" Val turned her gaze to Ria.

"He's obviously picking up on the icy atmosphere in the room, but if you ask your sister-in-law nicely, she might let you hold Jon." Ria smiled again, although her eyes did not.

"Huh! Arla and I stopped speaking a long time ago." Val tossed her head and folded her arms.

"No Val, you stopped speaking to me; God knows why." Arla continued pacing.

"Actually I think it was the other way around." Val's lips set in a firm line.

"Oh for goodness sake!" Ria shook her head in exasperation at Val. "My hormones are all over the place; the last thing I want is any arguments on what is supposed to be a happy occasion. If you can't reconcile your differences with Arla, then I must ask you to leave."

"Fair enough." Val stood up. "Come on Mum; let's go." "Sit down Val." Edna commanded. "I'm starting to think this feud has gone on long enough. I'm not getting any younger; none of us are." She looked at her daughter. "Who knows who said what to whom? At this precise moment do you know what? I just don't *care*."

"Well I do." Val took her seat again reluctantly and addressed her mother. "She's wormed her way around Jan, and look at her now; purposely holding on to the baby so that you can't get a look in."

"Edna, would you like to hold Jon?" Arla ignored Val and walked towards her mother-in-law.

"Yes, I'd love to." Edna smiled and shuffled around to get more comfortable on the settee.

"He's an absolute peach." Arla bent over and placed the baby in her mother-in-law's arms. "Val, why on earth don't we try to get along and move on from this like reasonable adults?"

"He's a darling." Edna sighed as she cuddled the baby. "I'm happy to draw a line under the whole thing."

"Sounds good to me. What about you, Val?" Arla stood back up and faced her sister-in-law.

For the first time in her life, she saw that Val was lost for words and looked decidedly ill-at-ease.

"I don't think so. Too much water has gone under the bridge. Arla, we don't even like each other! I would only be pretending. I know you can't stand the sight of me, and the feeling is mutual. Anybody who disrespects my mother has got it coming from me." Val tossed her hair, shrugged, and looked over at the baby. "He's lovely, Ria."

"Thank you. My son needs to know that there's harmony in his life. He can't be doing with all this unhappiness." Ria took a cup of tea from Stuart, who had come in from the kitchen. "And to be quite honest, neither can I. Thanks for the tea, darling."

"My pleasure." Stuart moved baby paraphernalia to one side and placed a laden tray on the coffee table.

"Sugar, Val?" Arla handed over a cup of tea from the tray and felt like pouring the container of sweet cubes over her sister-in-law's head.

"No thanks." Val looked as if she had tasted something bitter.

"Well, let it be known that I've tried but failed to heal the rift this afternoon. Edna, I'm glad that, like me, you're prepared to let bygones be bygones. As you said, who cares what's been said over the years; we need to make up for lost time. Perhaps you'd like to come and visit with us more often? I'm sure Ric would want that too."

"Yes, I'd like that." Edna nodded. "I'm too old to fight anymore."

"Would you like some sugar in your coffee?" Arla felt like pinching herself in disbelief.

"Yeah; perhaps I could do with some sweetening up." Edna smiled. "God knows, I can be a *bitch* sometimes."

"It's forgotten." Arla disregarded the understatement, and smiled. "Do you know something, Stu?"

"What?" Stuart put a cup of sweetened coffee next to Edna on a side table.

"I'll say it again; you really have quite a remarkable wife!"

"I know." Stuart chuckled.

Arla smiled at her son and felt a sudden inner sadness for all the lost years when she could have made more of an effort to get along with Ric's family. However, she was thankful to have been given a second chance to befriend Edna, which was due in no uncertain terms to the combined efforts of Toni Beecher, coupled with the kind nature and astuteness of Ria, her special daughter-in-law. There and then Arla determined to don her thinking cap and devise a plan to get around the prickly, pitiless Val.

She realised that her mother had been right all those years ago to make her share her toys with her best friend. Arla had found out just in time that the cure for every shred of bitterness, jealousy and hatred she had ever felt could be found within herself, and in the long run all that was needed was a loving and forgiving heart.

CHAPTER 39

ARLA LET GO of Jon's fingers, left him buckled into his baby seat and jumped out of the back of Ria's car. As she opened the front passenger door she mused on how in the whole of her married life she had never gone shopping with her mother-in-law. Today was the first occasion that Edna had asked to accompany them without Val or Jan, in order to buy her great-grandson a first birthday present.

"Okay?" Arla noticed her mother-in-law's slow movements. "Do you need any help?"

"No; I don't think so thanks."

Arla sighed inwardly as proud, stiff Edna struggled to get out of the car. She clocked Ria's laughing eyes on the other side of the car as her daughter-in-law opened the back door to unbuckle Jon, and realised that the shopping expedition would probably take up most of the day. She had no idea if Val or Jan ever offered their arm up for Edna to hold, and wondered if she should make the announcement that hers was free to cling onto.

"I'm here if you need an arm, Edna."

"I'll remember that."

When Jon was safely ensconced in his pushchair, the old lady started to walk at a snail's pace along the pavement, dogged in her determination not to be seen out in public using any walking aids. The shopping centre was at least another 10 minutes' walk from the car park; maybe half an hour at Edna's pace. Suddenly Arla had a flash of inspiration and winked at Ria over Edna's head:

"Would you like to push your great-grandson?" Arla kept her voice light and cheery. "I bet you haven't pushed a pram in years!"

"I haven't, no." Edna agreed. "Yes, okay. It would be like old times again."

With her mother-in-law somewhat more stable holding onto a pseudo-frame and walking a bit faster, Arla felt she could relax more and not worry about the old lady falling over. She was quite pleased at having thought up the idea, and as they waited for the lift down into the main road she started to think that maybe the expedition would be a success.

Ria took a piece of peeled apple out of a plastic container and gave it to her son:

"What would you like to buy him, Granny?"

Arla was amazed at the familiarity between Edna and Ria. In all the time she had known Edna she had never thought of calling her anything other than her name. However, Ria had no qualms, and had soon copied her husband's familiar address of his grandmother.

"Something to wear perhaps?" Edna puffed slightly with the effort of pushing the pram. "Is he growing out of most of his clothes?"

"He is." Ria nodded. "Clothes would be good. Shall we go to Mothercare?"

"Okay." Edna looked about the shopping centre. "Which way?"

"Over there." Arla pointed along the main road towards the indoor shopping centre. "When we're done we can have a cup of tea and a doughnut in Greggs on the first floor if you like."

"I can't have doughnuts, they'll clog me up again." Edna shook her head. "I'll have the cup of tea though."

"Okay."

Mothercare was heaving with shoppers. Although it was not particularly cold for the end of October, the heating in the shop had been turned on full blast. Arla started to sweat. Ria steered Edna towards a rack containing tiny dungarees and matching t-shirts with motifs reading '*Mummy's little Prince*'.

"He'll look great in those." "Great-

Granny will get him some then."

Edna picked up a pair of dungarees and a tiny t-shirt, fumbled in her purse, and then pushed the pram towards the till. As she paid for her purchases, Ria peered in at Jon and pulled a face.

"Oh, I think we have what Stu politely calls a 'Code Brown'. It must have been that apple."

"Do they have a mother's room?" Arla looked towards the back of the shop. "Ah yes, I can see one. If you go and change Jon, Edna and I will go up to Greggs."

"Okay, see you there."

Without the pram to hold onto, Edna's pace slowed. Arla could see that the old lady was rather too frail to be traipsing around huge shopping centres, but could only admire Edna's determination to walk unaided. There was an escalator up to the first floor, and Arla's heart was in her mouth as Edna walked towards it.

When she thought back and related the tale to Ric, it was as though the accident had happened in slow motion. She watched Edna step gingerly onto the first rung of the escalator, but realised too late that her mother-in-law's aged reflexes were not quick enough to enable her to grab the handrail in time. Arla, standing behind Edna on the escalator, was too late to steady her, and a kind of horrible, unreal moment ensued as the old lady fell forwards onto the moving staircase with a dull thud, cracking her forehead on the steel steps whilst all the time travelling upwards towards the first floor.

Thankfully somebody, Arla never found out who it was, pushed the emergency stop button. The escalator ground to a halt as Edna neared the end of the ride. Arla, bending over Edna, could see that the old lady had suffered a blow to the head and was concussed.

"We need an ambulance!" Her voice came out thin and reedy as she searched in her bag for a mobile phone. "She's been knocked out!"

A passing teenager on the first floor signalled to confirm he had called the paramedics. Edna lay still and silent on the escalator. People behind Arla turned around and walked back to the ground floor, and somebody came out of one of the upper level homeware shops carrying some blankets and a pillow.

Arla, crouching down beside Edna on the narrow escalator, was relieved to see the old lady starting to come round, groaning and incoherent, but thankfully alive. Blood had spattered over the step from an egg-shaped lump on her forehead. She covered her with a blanket, lifted up her head slightly, and placed it back down on a pillow.

"You're alright, Edna." She took hold of her mother-in-law's hand. "You've had a fall; the ambulance is on its way."

She looked over the handrail and could see a concerned Ria looking up at her, and Jon asleep in the pushchair. She managed to convey what had occurred to Ria, just as the paramedics burst through the main doors, burdened under the weight of equipment they were carrying.

"Up here!" She waved. "Ria! I'm going in the ambulance with Edna!"

She saw her daughter-in-law nodding and then making her way in the direction of the car park. She moved out of the way to allow the two paramedics to check Edna over before they lifted her onto a collapsible stretcher, and then she followed them down the escalator into the waiting ambulance.

The lights in the ambulance were bright, making Arla blink. Edna lay pale and dazed on the stretcher. One of the paramedics started the engine, and the other checked her vital signs. Arla sat in the corner opposite trying to keep the old lady alert.

"Edna, it's Arla here. Can you hear me?" She took hold of the old, veined hand again.

"Wha……?"

"Don't go to sleep; you must stay awake!"

"Ahhhh…….."

The amount of equipment inside the ambulance caused a permanent rattle as it sped along the main road. The movement caused Edna to begin vomiting. The paramedic sat her up while Arla held the kidney dish. Arla, feeling queasy herself with the delayed shock, gave the bowl to the paramedic to dispose of after he had laid Edna down.

"Don't worry, Edna, I'm still here."

By the time they reached the hospital Arla could see Edna was more awake. She walked to the side of the stretcher into Accident and Emergency, all the while making sure that Edna could see her. As they went straight through into Triage, she felt grateful to be able to sit down and let the medics take over.

The Medical Admission Unit was only half full. Arla sat by Edna's bed as the old lady looked at her and smiled.

"Thanks for staying with me. I don't know what happened."

"You fell on the escalator at the shopping centre. Do you remember?"

"Vaguely." Edna wracked her brain. "I must have lost my footing."

"Something like that." Arla refrained from stating the true problem. "They're going to keep you in overnight because you were knocked out."

"Oh, such a bother!" Edna sighed. "I'll be alright. Why – I think that's Ria coming in, isn't it?"

Arla turned around and waved:

"Yes, she took Jon back to the car and drove here. Hi Ria! Did you get through to Val or Jan?"

"Yes, both of them." Ria put the brakes on the pushchair and checked her phone. "I've just had a text from Jan to say she's on her way.

"I don't need them fussing around." Edna shook her head. "Arla's done fine on her own."

Arla felt a pleasant *frisson* of acceptance running through her veins for the first time.

"I didn't really do much." She smiled at her mother-in-law.

"Nonsense; of course you did." Edna patted Arla's hand. "Where would I have been without you?"

CHAPTER 40

AS SHE HAD expected, within half an hour of Ria's arrival Arla heard Val's strident tones floating across from the reception desk. She took great pleasure in knowing that herself and Ria were taking up the only two visitor chairs, and that Val would have to stand.

"Mum! What's been going on?"

Arla was aware that Val was trying to get nearer to her mother in the bed, by trying to push past her in the process. She stayed firmly in her chair and refused to move her legs out of the way. If Val was going to ignore her, then Arla surmised that two could play that game. Edna waved away her daughter's question and turned to Arla.

"Never you mind; Arla's been looking after me just fine."

Arla was surprised to feel Edna patting her hand again. She gloated inwardly at Val's obvious displeasure as her sister-in-law tried to assert her authority over the situation.

"What on earth were you doing? You know you shouldn't go traipsing round shopping centres!"

"I asked to go. I wanted to get a present for Jon, so don't blame Arla or Ria. I just slipped on the escalator, that's all. Don't make a fuss." Edna sniffed. "It could have happened to anybody."

Arla's face registered no emotion as one thought crossed her mind.

Yeah it could have happened to anybody, but probably more likely would happen to tottery old people over the age of eighty who refuse to use a stick……

"You can go now, Arla. Thanks, but I'll stay with Mum."

Arla thought Val looked as though she had a bad smell under her nose. She stayed put in her chair and answered Val in a non-confrontational voice.

"I can only go when Ria's ready. She'll give me a lift to the station."

"I've only just got here." Ria smiled sweetly at Val. Edna, sporting a blood-spattered bandage on her head, sat up in bed and took control of the situation.

"Val, for goodness sake, go and bring a chair and sit down."

A silence had descended. Arla was conscious that she was sitting in the prime spot next to Edna, Val was irritable at being seated near the end of the bed, and Ria rocked a sleeping Jon backwards and forwards in the pushchair, seemingly other-worldly and oblivious. Arla desperately tried to think of something to say, but at the last moment Edna beat her to it.

"Oh God, that's all we need; now Jan's arrived. Who else did you call, Ria?"

"Just Jan and Val." Ria shrugged as she rocked. "The boys are all at work."

"Mum! What's happened?" Jan squeezed past her sister and sat down on the edge of the bed by Arla.

"If you don't stop making a fuss I'm going to discharge meself." Edna sighed. "Just thank Arla that she was on hand to help me out."

"It was nothing." Arla smiled. "I didn't do much actually."

"Thanks." Jan gave Arla a quick hug and sat back down on the bed. "Thanks for looking after Mum."

"You should be grateful too, Val." Ria stopped rocking the pram. "All you've said to Arla is to ask her to go home."

Arla, embarrassed, wanted the floor to swallow her up. She signalled to Ria with a tiny shake of the head, but realised with horror that her daughter-in-law was only just getting into her stride.

"I don't know what your problem is with Arla, but I'd really like to find what it is. Perhaps then we can find a way to sort it out, and then all relax and forget about it." Ria fixed Val with a steely gaze.

"I haven't got a problem with Arla." Val met Ria's stare with one of her own.

"Then why are you constantly walking around as though you've got a squib up your arse every time you see her?"

"I beg your pardon?" Val's eyes burned into Ria's face.

"You heard me. We're going to sort it out now. I'm cheesed off with it all." Ria's voice began to rise. "Arla's busted her gut to help Granny, and you can't even say thanks."

"Ria….." Arla's face burned. "Leave it. It's no good; you're flogging a dead horse."

"Then I'll flog it some more." Ria leaned forward towards Val for extra effect and hissed through clenched teeth. "*What. Is. Your. Problem?!* I was brought up in love and harmony, and want the same for my son. I want to have family get-togethers with no awkward atmosphere that everyone picks up on and talks about afterwards."

"Yes, Val, what *is* your problem?" Edna leaned back on the pillows. "Arla and I have sorted our differences. We might as well get it out in the open while we're all sitting here with nothing to do."

Val tore her eyes away from Ria for a split second, and looked over at her mother:

"With everything that's gone on over the years, and the way she's treated you, Mum, I'm afraid I just don't like her." She looked back at Ria. "I'm sure there are people in this world Ria, that even *you* don't like."

"Yes, but only one." Ria stood up. "*You.* Come on Arla, I'll give you a lift back to catch your train."

As she walked off the ward with Ria, Arla turned to her and smiled:

"Thanks for the support, but leave it trying to make a difference with Val; you'll never get anywhere."

"That's where you're wrong." Ria shook her head. "Giving up is not in my nature. There *is* a way forward; we've just got to think of it."

CHAPTER 41

AT LEAST THE sun had come out from behind the clouds. She had always thought there was nothing worse than standing in the rain by an open grave. Arla, trying to stay in the background under a shady yew tree, rocked the pushchair to and fro in which three-year-old Jon slept, whilst watching a hugely pregnant Ria joining Shelley, Dave, Val, Jan and their families in the front row of mourners by the graveside.

She felt awkward standing there without Ric, and preferred to take a back seat and look after her grandson. She wondered if Val really wanted her there at all, but Ric had suddenly turned masterful and reminded her that she was part of the family and it was her duty to attend.

It was quite peculiar; in the two weeks since his mother had passed on after her final heart attack she had noticed Ric suddenly starting to express a choice; not in an overly forthright manner, but quietly stating his preferences, not only to her, but also to his sisters and brothers-in-law. She found it quite refreshing to hear him state a genuine opinion, and did not mind at all that it was often the complete opposite to her own.

She looked at Ric, Stuart, Ben and Mark as they walked along shoulder to shoulder with the undertakers, each bearing a part of the burdensome oak coffin. Their eyes were dry, and their faces remained expressionless. Arla glanced over at the mourners by the graveside watching the coffin's arrival; not one person was visibly upset. She hoped when it was time for her own funeral that at the very least there would be perhaps just one person sniffing into a tissue, sad to see her disappear into the bowels of the earth.

Jon began to stir. Arla pushed the pram along a gravel path between some old, mildewed tombstones and a newer collection of graves, some still just mounds of earth. Edna was joining the new set whether she liked it or not, having no pre-paid funeral plans or family burial plot. Ric had already shown her his father's grave, recognisable by one of the older, more weathered tombstones across the other side of the path. Arla chuckled; the pair would be destined to forever flit across the gravel at midnight to meet up, unless the old boy had been having too good a time in the hereafter to want to recall his earlier, earthly life with her less-than-saintly mother-in-law.

The coffin was positioned over the grave, and the casket-lowering straps were put in place. Arla could not quite hear the priest's platitudes, and wondered how many of the mourners were actually listening to his words. She saw the undertakers gather up the straps and lower Edna into her final resting place, followed swiftly by Val stepping forward with her symbolic trowel of earth, and then Jan, and finally Ric and the rest of the grandchildren.

While the mourners chatted idly at the graveside after the service, she saw Ric head towards her, black tie already loosened:

"Well, the old girl's in the ground now."

"How do you feel?" Arla kept the pushchair in motion.

"You sound like that bloody counsellor."

"Sorry; it seemed to all go okay." "Yeah; do you know what?" "What?"

"It sounds awful, but for the first time in fifty two years I feel free." He lifted his face to the sun.

"I've often heard other people say the same thing after the loss of a loved one during my time as a nurse." Arla nodded.

"She wasn't a loved one; I was shit scared of her as a kid, but I don't think I ever loved her." Ric's eyes filled with tears. "Isn't it an awful thing to say about your own mother? I never loved her, yet she had some sort of hold over me I couldn't escape from." He shuddered and wiped his eyes.

"Well, I think it was all to do with your dad dying the way he did and the guilt you felt about it. Shall we go over to your dad's grave? The hearse won't be leaving just yet."

Leaving their grandson in the capable hands of his mother, Arla slipped her hand in Ric's and together they crossed the path towards the older side of the cemetery, coming to a halt before a tombstone reading *'Patrick Lewis Deane, born December 16th 1929, died April 27th 1977'. Rest in Peace.*

"You don't know how much I've longed for him to come back over the years." Ric sighed and shook his head. "I never told him how much I loved him."

"You're telling him now." Arla rested her head against his arm. "Wherever he is, I'm sure he can hear you."

"Why did he have to die so young?" Ric shook his head.

"It was his time to go; there's nothing anyone could have done about it." She kissed his cheek.

"I love you; I don't know where I'd be without you." Ric rested his head on hers.

"You're not without me; you'll never be without me, so don't worry about it."

They stood in silence in front of the grave until it was time to walk back to the waiting hearse.

CHAPTER 42

"I'VE AGREED WITH Val and Jan that the six grandchildren can come round and see if there's any furniture of Mum's that they want, before I contact the council to come and take it away."

Ric turned the key in the lock, and Arla could still smell a faint whiff of Edna's perfume when he pushed the door open. She almost expected to see the old lady walking up the hallway to greet them, but there was no sound except for the grandfather clock chiming the hour.

"Stu and Ria could do with her dining table and chairs, that's for sure." Arla nodded. "Ben and Marie have just got married; I'm sure they'll be grateful for anything. Did she make a will?"

"No; there was never any mention of one. The council's given us two weeks leeway to clear the house before they move the next tenant in. We'd better make a start. Val and Jan have taken the mementos they want, but don't fancy going through all her things; it's all down to me." Ric sighed. "Thanks for your help darling."

"It's the least I can do. Where do you want me to start?" Arla shivered in the July heat, wanting to be out of the house as soon as possible."

"The Skip's arrived now. Perhaps start with her clothes? If there's anything nice perhaps it can be bagged up for the charity shop; anything old can just go in the Skip." Ric looked around and sighed again. "This is the house I grew up in; it doesn't seem possible that someone else will be living in it soon. Out in the back garden is where Dad died; God, what an awful job this is." He ran a hand distractedly through his hair.

"Come on darling, the sooner we get cracking the sooner it'll be over." Arla kissed him briefly. "I'll go upstairs and clear out the bedrooms."

The duvet was pulled back on the bed from where the undertakers had carried Edna off in a body bag. Arla stripped the bed and bundled the bedclothes into black sacks. The digital clock by the bedside still showed the right time, and the alarm was set for six thirty. Arla unplugged the clock, but left it on the mattress in case one of the grandchildren came around to claim it. Family photos in frames stood on the bedside cabinet next to an array of pills, and with some surprise she noticed a photograph of herself and Richard when they were first married. She picked up the photo and turned it over; on the back of the frame Edna had written '1982'.

The four wardrobes were stuffed full of clothes, mostly old-fashioned and moth-eaten. Arla filled up ten black sacks with Edna's jumpers, skirts and suits, and threw them down the stairs to rest by the front door. She checked the empty wardrobes, and satisfied, moved on to the dressing table. She was surprised at the small amount of jewellery her mother-in-law possessed, and laid it out carefully on the mattress for Val and Jan to deliberate over. As she started to gather up various items of make-up from the dressing table drawer, she saw an envelope hidden underneath a large powder compact. When she brought it out into the light to get a better view of the writing on the front, she saw that Edna had written *'To Arla, my daughter-in-law'* in a shaky hand.

Heart thumping, she carefully tore open the envelope. The letter was dated two months before Edna's death, and Arla could see by the writing how frail the old lady had become. She unfolded a sheet of lilac-coloured paper, which had been part of a writing set she remembered buying for her mother-in-law the previous Christmas:

'Dear Arla,

I hope you'll find this letter. My health is failing, and I don't know how much time I've got left. I know Val and Jan won't want to look through all my things after I'm gone, but you're made of sterner stuff. How do I know? Because you're just like me; not to look at, but the personality's the same.

I saw the resemblance as soon as Ric brought you home that time. He'd found a girl just like his mother, as many men do of course. I am ashamed to admit I was envious of you for many years for taking him from me, and I realise I must have made your life hell. I didn't come to my senses until Stu and Ria's wedding, when I saw what a good relationship you had with your own daughter-in -law, free of the jealousy and bitterness which has overshadowed the two of us. I hope you will forgive me for all the lost years when I treated you so badly.

My son chose his wife wisely, and your children are a credit to you. I'm so sorry for how I've behaved, but cannot write more at the moment. Yours, Edna x'

The piece of paper bore traces of the perfume she could smell throughout the house. Arla sighed with the sure and certain knowledge that she had behaved just as badly towards her mother-in-law; the bitter feelings had only been partly alleviated in recent years as the old lady's health had declined and with the birth of Jon.

She felt a great sadness descend upon her, and her eyes misted over with tears. Sitting at Edna's dressing table, she was suddenly grateful to Toni and Ria for their insight into the complexities of human interactions; of course she, Arla, had no right at all to have even thought about interfering in her son's choice of life partner. Stuart had only been on loan to her for a short time; he was now an adult in his own right, capable of making his own decisions, and it was only natural that he would want to find happiness and that the mother/child bond should loosen as the years went on. She had found out just in time what it took Edna over thirty years to discover; *at the end of the day, jealousy will get you nowhere.*

She smiled as she folded the letter carefully and placed it in her bag. She had finally found the missing piece of the jigsaw.

CHAPTER 43

ARLA PRESSED A button on the remote control to mute the TV sound.

"You need to invite Val round here for a meal and then go down the pub or something. I need to speak to her."

"Why don't *you* do it then?" Ric, channel hopping, was lending only half an ear.

"Because she won't come if I invite her; you know that."

"What do you want to speak to her about?" "Everything, anything; I don't know. Can you give her a call please?

"She'll think it strange if I bugger off as soon as she gets here."

"Well stay then if you want."

"I'd better; her claws will be out as soon as she sees you."

"Just phone her and leave the rest to me."

Feeling less nervous than she thought she might, she sat stiffly on the settee and let Ric open the door. She could hear Val's voice protesting almost straight away.

"Why have I been summoned here?"

Ric's reply was muffled; gentle and wheedling. Arla smiled as her sister-in-law came into view.

"Hi, Val. It was me who asked you here. Ric, could you make us some tea, please?"

Arla watched as Val took the seat furthest away from her and looked at her questioningly:

"What's the problem?"

"There's no problem." Arla shook her head. "It's just that I wanted you to see a note that Edna wrote to me. I found it when Ric and I were clearing out her things."

She unfolded the piece of paper from her pocket, stood up and placed it in Val's hand before returning to her seat. She scanned her sister-in-law's face intently as she read it, trying to gauge a reaction. However, Val's expression remained impassive, and she shrugged as she passed the note back.

"Mum was ill when she wrote that."

"Not too ill that she wasn't aware what she was writing. As far as I can tell she's apologising to me."

"So?" Val shrugged again.

"So…..what I'm trying to do here is to state to you that this long-standing feud between us hasn't been entirely my fault."

"What do you want – a medal then?" Val crossed one leg over the other and sighed.

"Come on Val, loosen up." Arla smiled. "I'm prepared to forgive and forget and move on. We can't spend the rest of our lives at loggerheads with each other."

"Can't we?"

"No, this is silly and childish. I don't even know what I've done to make you hate me so much."

"The way you treated my mother over the years leaves much to be desired." Val sniffed. "I think you actually enjoyed some of it."

"Maybe I did, but it was only in retaliation for what she was doing to *me*." Arla felt as though she wanted to scream in frustration. "Can't you see? She was jealous of me taking Ric away from her; she said so herself in the letter. Can you not see my side of the story for once? Forget that Edna was your mother for just a minute, and try and see both sides of the coin."

"I can't go against my own mother; it wouldn't be right." Val shook her head.

"Okay, but hopefully you can see that I gave out the same as I received. The bad feeling wasn't all one-sided. Thanks for the tea, Ric."

As her husband tactfully departed, Arla passed a cup to Val.

"How about a biscuit as well?"

"No thanks; I'll never fit into my skirts if I start eating those." Val took the cup from Arla.

"I've always envied you your slim figure." Arla smiled. "I never had the will-power you've got."

"It's easy; you just starve yourself." Val laughed ruefully. "I think a lifetime of it is starting to affect my bones though; I'm getting a touch of arthritis."

"Oh; most people our age have that." Arla tried to keep the conversation flowing but then could have kicked herself. "Sorry; didn't mean it to sound like you were getting old." She sighed.

"Well I am; let's face it. I'm pushing sixty."

"I'm not far behind you." Arla made a face. "I'm walking up Menopause Alley."

"I'm holding it off with my little pills." Val put her hands together in prayer. "God knows what I'd do if the GP stopped giving them out. I've been taking HRT for years."

"Really?" Arla sat up straighter with interest. "My doctor wouldn't prescribe them."

"I think the rationale has changed somewhat recently." Val sipped her tea. "They're frightened of breast cancer, but I'd rather have a boob off than hot flushes every half an hour."

"It sucks, doesn't it?" Arla agreed. "Sometimes I wish I'd been born a man."

"Then you'd get the old man's disease instead. Ronnie's in and out of the toilet all day. Actually, I sometimes want to lock him in there for good so that he can't get out."

Arla threw back her head and laughed:

"Thanks for coming here today, Val."

"That's okay; let me have another look at that note."

With a growing feeling hope that maybe her sister-in-law had started to thaw towards her, Arla fished it out of her pocket again. This time she noticed that Val read it more carefully.

"The old girl *was* difficult; sure." Val nodded. "After Dad died and Jan and I married, I think she would have liked Ric to stay around at home and keep her company; you know, like the youngest one used to do in Victorian times."

"I had wondered if it was something like that." Arla agreed. "Sure, it would be great to have your kids at your beck and call in your dotage, but we can't do that to them can we?"

"No, of course not. Ben and Mark would be horrified!" Val laughed. "I'm pleased for them though, that they've found nice girls; I must say your Ria's a great find."

"Yes, she's lovely." Arla smiled. "I must admit I suffered the same jealousies at first as Edna did when Ric met me. I even went for counselling. I'm glad I did; it made me confront my own faults. It's very hard to do." Arla screwed up her face. "I learned that you have to wave your kids goodbye and let them get on with their own lives."

"You speak a lot of sense. Mum couldn't let go." Val sighed.

"I know; Ric was torn between Edna and me for years."

"But if push came to shove, he would have chosen you I know, and that's what Mum hated." Val handed back the letter to Arla. "She couldn't stand having to be second best."

"Funnily enough that's what I always felt; that I came in a close second to Edna." Arla laughed. "It's the reason Ric and I went for counselling in the first place."

"Ric went too?" Val laughed out loud. "Oh God; I would have loved to have been a fly on the wall there!"

"Getting men to open up is like trying to squeeze blood out of the proverbial stone." Arla enjoyed the sudden camaraderie. "I had to almost get on my knees and beg him to accompany me. It did him good in the long run though; slayed a few ghosts so to speak."

"Ghosts?" Val cocked her head with interest.

"You know, the upset that occurred when your dad died."

"What upset?" Val put her empty cup down on the coffee table. "What are you talking about?"

"You know; Ric was there when he died. They were playing football. Your dad dropped dead in front of Ric." Arla looked behind her, but Ric was nowhere to be seen."

"No; that's not true!" Val shook her head. "Dad died in hospital; Mum told me!"

CHAPTER 44

ARLA NEEDED A sugar rush to deal with Val's revelation. Nibbling on a biscuit seemed to calm her somewhat.

"Were you there at the time?" Arla poured another cup of tea. "If you'd seen Ric break down, you'd have known he was telling the truth. I know he wouldn't lie about something like that."

"Jan and I were both out that day. I went with Mum later on to see him at the chapel of rest; Jan and Ric didn't want to go. Mum told me he'd had a heart attack at home but died in hospital." Val appeared confused.

"She must have not wanted Ric to be any more upset than he was. She was protecting him I expect." Arla looked at Val. "And probably didn't want you and Jan to know, otherwise you might have blamed Ric too, for making your dad run around when he wasn't a well man."

"We didn't know Dad was ill; no I would never have blamed Ric." Val shook her head in disbelief. "Just imagine; Mum lied to me all those years, her own daughter. I don't understand it."

"Can you see where I'm coming from?" Arla sat forward in her seat. "This is what I had to put up with for years! I know Edna also told you things about me which weren't true. You *know* I'm right, don't you? But I'm just the daughter-in-law; I didn't stand a chance against the three of you."

"Some of the things she came out with were a bit far-fetched I must admit." Val chuckled. "But as I said; she wanted to keep Ric at home for company. In the end she realised he wasn't coming home, but by then it was war. Nothing Jan or I could say or do would have made any difference. Can I have a biscuit please?"

"Sure; it'll make me feel better." Arla handed over the plate. "I'm going to have another one."

The two women smiled together conspiratorially over their tea and biscuits. Arla felt more confident that she was getting somewhere at last.

"I'm sorry if I upset Edna over the years. I found out a few things about myself during counselling, and I'm ashamed. I was young and silly when I met Ric, and decided to give back what I received. I should have understood her more and realised that she was lonely."

"She *was* a difficult lady." Val smiled. "But at the end of the day she was my mum, and I loved her. You don't have the insight when you're young; it takes pushing sixty to realise all this. I think I must have realised that a lot of what she said about you wasn't true, but like Jan, we didn't want to upset her."

"Forget it now." Arla waved Val's admission away. "It's all water under the bridge. What I need to know is that we can move on from this and become friends."

"Absolutely." Val nodded. "I'm game if you are."

"It's a deal!" Arla jumped out of her chair and gave Val a spontaneous hug. "Do you know what? You've made my day!"

The time flew away as they talked about days gone by. When Val eventually left for home most of the afternoon had disappeared. Arla was aware that Ric had remained tactfully absent during his sister's visit, only appearing in order to say goodbye. When she followed him out into the kitchen she was delighted to find out that he had prepared two ham and egg salads for their dinner.

"Lovely!" She kissed him. "Thanks for giving us the chance to talk today."

"You two seemed to be getting on like a house on fire at the end. It's great."

He put his arms around her. "I can't cook, but salads are not beyond me; well, not yet anyway."

"She even invited me to join her and Jan on a girly weekend away somewhere. It's bizarre! And do you know what else, she and Jan had no idea about the circumstances of your dad's death. Your mum told them he died in hospital."

"Oh God, you weren't talking about that, were you?" He looked horrified as he held her at arm's length. "I want to try and forget about it."

"It was good to get it out in the open; somehow it forged the bond between us that wasn't there before. She was shocked that Edna had lied to her all those years ago; it brought home to her how *I'd* been treated. She admitted that Edna often made up awful stories to Val and Jan about me in the hope that you'd get to hear about them and believe your mother, causing me to run off and leave you still staying at home with her instead."

"No way; she would have driven me mad!" Ric chuckled. "If that was her plan then she went the wrong way about it."

"Oh?" Arla put her arms around Ric's waist and her head on his chest. "What should she have done then?

"To make me stay at home?"

"Yeah."

"There was nothing she could have done. I grew up and it was time for me to go, although if she'd have taken Farrah Fawcett-Majors in as a lodger at the time, then I might have stayed a bit longer…"

Arla playfully pinched his behind:

"I can't come close to Farrah, but I can pout and toss my hair about a bit if you like?"

"That'll do. Come on; eat your salad. I've slaved away in this kitchen all bloody afternoon."

The salad was surprisingly well presented and tasty. As she bit into a slice of ham, Arla thought how delicious food could be when somebody else prepared it.

CHAPTER 45

THERE WAS SOMETHING decadent about swanning around in a dressing gown in the middle of the day. Arla tried to remember the last time she had eaten lunch clad in a towelling robe, and came to the conclusion that it must have been when her children were newborns.

"I feel as though I should get dressed." She looked across the table at Val and Jan. "This doesn't seem right somehow."

"Chill! Make the most of it; it's what Clarence House is all about. After our massages this afternoon you can relax by the pool if you like, or you can come with us and have your toenails done." Val's tinkly laugh carried around the room. "Jan and I have been coming here for years."

"That'll be a first for me; I've never given it a thought that somebody else might want to paint my toenails." Arla giggled as she nibbled at a tasty nut roast.

"I'm having a bikini wax as well." Jan interjected. "Treat yourself and give Ric a thrill."

"Sounds painful." Arla laughed. "I might pass on that one and go swimming instead. Thanks for inviting me along though; it's a great place here."

"Yeah." Jan agreed. "We can get away from all the men for a whole weekend. We come back feeling twenty years younger, although it's best not to look in the mirror to confirm that."

"Age is just a number." Arla nodded. "You're as old as you feel."

"Right now I feel about seventeen." Val giggled. "I've had my legs waxed, my eyelashes tinted, a cut and blow dry, and a colonic."

"Ronnie had better look out tomorrow night then." Jan remarked drily.

"I'm safe with his prostate the way it is." Val sighed. "If I wanted a bit I'd have to go and sit on the toilet with him."

"He needs to go to the doctor." Arla took a sip of wine and looked at Val. "I'll get Ric to read him the riot act if you like."

"You know what men are like." Val rolled her eyes to the heavens. "Anything to do with the wedding tackle and they're in denial."

"Ric and Ronnie go way back; if anyone could persuade him it might be Ric." Arla nodded to confirm her suggestion.

"Sure; thanks. You never know…..let's hope!"

Laid out half naked and face down on the massage table like a plucked chicken and with her head pushed down inside a kind of towelled hole, Arla wanted to giggle. In the cubicle next door she could hear Val confidently instructing the masseuse which parts of her body to work on, and from somewhere opposite she could hear Jan's muted snoring.

"Where shall I concentrate today?" The masseuse warmed up her hands. "I'm just going to apply some grapeseed oil to your back."

"The lower back please." Arla thought her voice sounded as though she was sitting in a bucket. "That gives me the most trouble."

"Okay, but I'll also work on the top of your back as well though; all the muscles feel stiff actually."

"Just do your thing." Arla felt slightly claustrophobic inside the hole. "How long do you think it'll take?"

"About half an hour."

As the masseuse began working on her back, Arla started to relax and to zone out on the sounds going on around her. Thoughts meandered idly around her head; she would never have believed that she could be at a health spa with her two sisters-in-law and be enjoying the experience so much. She had found Jan's rather dry sense of humour to be similar to her own, and underneath Val's gruff exterior there seemed to be a kind person trying to get out. She tried not to think about all the wasted years of backbiting and jealousy.

"Hey Arla! How are you getting on?"

Val's voice soared over the cubicle curtains, waking Jan up in the process, who snorted loudly.

"Alright, I think." Arla grinned into the hole. "It's quite relaxing actually."

"I've been asleep." Jan yawned.

"Yeah, we could hear." Val replied.

"Oh no, was I snoring?" Jan giggled.

"Like a barrack room full of soldiers." Arla decided to join in, where previously she would have held back. "It was awesome."

"I'm embarrassed!" Jan trilled.

"Forget it." Arla laughed. "I'll probably be doing the same in a minute."

Feeling surprisingly refreshed after her massage, Arla decided to follow Val and Jan into the nail clinic.

"Have you really never painted your toenails?" Val looked at her in astonishment.

"No; who's going to see them?" Arla looked down at her feet in their white throwaway slippers. "Only Ric, and he probably wouldn't notice anyway. He hates feet."

"You've got the wrong idea; have it done for *you*." Jan remarked with a grin. "As Val said, you'll come out of here feeling years younger. He'll be sucking your toes tonight."

"Ewww… I do hope not." Arla could not think of anything worse. "I'll miss that scene if you don't mind."

"Adie always massages my feet." Jan kept a straight face. "It says it turns him on."

"Ronnie's never out of the toilet long enough to suck my toes." Val sighed. "Perhaps I can suck his though, while he's sitting on the bog."

Sunday evening came too soon, and Arla was certain that she had never laughed so much ever before in one weekend.Reluctantly she added her towelling robe to the 'used' pile, but decided to keep the throwaway slippers as a kind of memento. She felt strange dressed in her outdoor clothes again.

"We'll have to do this often." She smiled at Val and Jan. "I've had a great time."

"Absolutely; Jan and I usually go after the Christmas mayhem is over; that'll be the next one." Val threw her robe after Arla's, and gave her a hug.

"Include me in!" Arla nodded. "After all these years it's great having a couple of sisters!"

"Never think again that you're an only child." Jan smiled. "You're one of us now. Welcome to the family!"

THE END

If you have enjoyed this book, you may wish to check out 'Lily: A Short Story', also by Stevie Turner.

Review of Lily: A Short Story

"One of the best books I've read all year. Lily--a beautiful person who suffered many tragedies in her lifetime. The writer had the uncanny knack of putting a reader right in the middle of the story. I felt so close to them. The ending is one of the most beautiful and moving finishes I have ever encountered. If I had to label it, I'd say that it was soulful. I know it left quite an impact on me. Excellent!" - *Carole McKee*

Other Works by Stevie Turner

The Pilates Class
A House Without Windows
Lily: A Short Story
No Sex Please, I'm Menopausal!
For the Sake of a Child
A Rather Unusual Romance
Revenge
Repent at Leisure
The Donor
Life: 18 Short Stories
Waiting in the Wings
Mind Games
Leg-less and Chalaza
Alys in Hunger-land
Cruising Danger
A Marriage of Convenience

CPSIA information can be obtained
at www.ICGtesting.com
Printed in the USA
LVHW041147201119
637825LV00005B/370/P